A LITTLE EASTER DELIGHT

LAYLAH ROBERTS

LET'S KEEP IN TOUCH!

Don't miss a new release by signing up to my newsletter. You'll get sneak peeks, deleted scenes, and giveaways: https://landing. mailerlite.com/webforms/landing/p7l6g0

You can also join my Facebook readers' group here: https://www.facebook.com/groups/386830425069911/

BOOKS BY LAYLAH ROBERTS

Doms of Decadence

Just for You, Sir

Forever Yours, Sir

For the Love of Sir

Sinfully Yours, Sir

Make me, Sir

A Taste of Sir

To Save Sir

Sir's Redemption

Reveal Me, Sir

Montana Daddies

Daddy Bear

Daddy's Little Darling

Daddy's Naughty Darling Novella

Daddy's Sweet Girl

Daddy's Lost Love

A Montana Daddies Christmas

Daring Daddy

Warrior Daddy

Daddy's Angel

Heal Me, Daddy

Daddy in Cowboy Boots

A Little Christmas Cheer (crossover with MC Daddies)

Sheriff Daddy

Her Daddies' Saving Grace

Rogue Daddy

A Little Winter Wonderland

Daddy's Sassy Sweetheart

Daddy Dominic

Daddy Unleashed

MC Daddies

Motorcycle Daddy

Hero Daddy

Protector Daddy

Untamed Daddy

Her Daddy's Jewel

Fierce Daddy

A Little Christmas Cheer (crossover with Montana Daddies)

Savage Daddy

Boss Daddy

Daddy Fox

A Snowy Little Christmas

Saving Daddy

Daddies' Captive

A Foxy Little Christmas

A Little Easter Delight

Harem of Daddies

Ruled by her Daddies

Claimed by her Daddies

Stolen by her Daddies

Captured by her Daddies

Kept by her Daddies

Haven, Texas Series

Lila's Loves

Laken's Surrender

Saving Savannah

Molly's Man

Saxon's Soul

Mastered by Malone

How West was Won

Cole's Mistake

Jardin's Gamble

Romanced by the Malones

Twice the Malone

Mending a Malone

Malone's Heart

Malone's Pride

Malone's Fate

New Orleans Malones

Damaged Princess

Vengeful Commander

Wicked Prince

Men of Orion

Worlds Apart

Cavan Gang

Rectify

Redemption

Redemption Valley

Audra's Awakening

Old-Fashioned Series

An Old-Fashioned Man

Two Old-Fashioned Men

Her Old-Fashioned Husband

Her Old-Fashioned Boss

His Old-Fashioned Love

An Old-Fashioned Christmas

Crime Boss Daddies

Daddy's Obsession

Papi's Protection

Papi's Savior

Bad Boys of Wildeside

Wilde

Sinclair

Luke

Rawhide Ranch Holiday

A Cozy Little Christmas

A Little Easter Escapade

Standalones

Their Christmas Baby

Haley Chronicles

Ally and Jake

1

"Daddy! Daddy! I made my first invite! Isn't it adorable?" Millie came to a stop in front of Spike who was sitting on the sofa. Mr. Fluffy was sleeping on his bed next to Spike's feet. He opened one eye and stared up at her before falling back asleep.

"Don't worry, Mr. Fluffy, I have your outfit all ready. You are going to look so adorable for our super-duper Easter egg hunt!!" She went to clap her hands before she remembered the invitation she was holding.

Oops. She had to be careful! She didn't want to ruin the surprise.

Carefully, she handed it over to Spike. "Take a look, Daddy!"

"Cute," he said.

The invitation looked like an Easter egg resting on a flat base, and it was all glittery and delicious.

"Open it, Daddy!"

He raised an eyebrow.

"Please. I want to make sure it works. The invitation part is inside the egg."

"How many people are coming to this thing?" he asked.

"It's not a *thing*. It's an amazing, super-duper awesome Easter egg hunt." She held her arms up dramatically.

Spike's lips twitched. "My apologies."

Millie patted his shoulder. "You'll get there, Daddy. Soon you'll be as excited as me. Isn't Easter the best?"

"I thought Christmas was the best?" he asked.

"It is!"

"And Valentine's Day?"

She nodded enthusiastically. "Also the best."

"How about Halloween?" he asked.

"Yep. Spooky best." She waved her fingers in the air. "Oooh. Oohh."

"What was that?" he asked.

"Um, the sound a ghost makes."

"Isn't that boo?"

"Pfft. That's too obvious."

"Ahh. So what about your birthday?"

"Best day of the year!"

He snorted. "So, how many people are coming?"

"Well, I have to send the invites first to get back the RSVPs. So I'm not sure," she told him.

Spike eyed her for a long moment. "Baby doll."

"Daddio!" she said back with a grin.

"No."

"No, what?" she asked.

"No to Daddio. I'm Daddy."

"You sure are. Do you know what sort of Daddy you are?" she asked.

He gave her a suspicious look. "No."

"The best Daddy!" she cried, arms in the air again.

"Yeah, nice try at distracting me. I still want to know how many people you're expecting."

"Hmm. Okay." She used her fingers to start counting. When she got to around thirty, he held his hand up.

"No. Just no."

"You say no a lot, Daddy. We need to expand your vocabulary."

"To what? Nope. Nuh-uh. No freaking way?"

"Hmm. That's an okay start. But I was kind of thinking more like, 'yes, of course, baby,' and 'whatever you want whenever you want,' and 'all I want is to make you happy.'"

"Um, still no. Send less invites."

"I can't!"

He gave her a stern look.

"Okay . . . okay . . . I'll cap it at thirty."

He sighed.

"Open it, Daddy. Please!" she cried.

"Fine."

He opened the invitation.

It exploded in a sea of glitter. Shades of blue, green, and red rained down on Spike's head, shoulders, and chest.

Millie placed her hand over her mouth, trying to stifle her giggles. But she couldn't stop them from escaping. They burst out of her as she stared at Spike.

He just sat there, staring at her, still as a statue.

Mr. Fluffy let out one woof and she glanced down to find that he had glitter on his nose. He opened his eyes for a brief moment, then heaved a huge sigh before rolling over onto his side.

Mr. Fluffy was used to her by now.

"What was that?" Spike asked in a low, controlled voice.

"Glitter bomb invitation! Isn't it the best?" She clapped her hands, bouncing up and down. "So. Much. Fun."

"Millie," he said in a low voice.

"Yes, Daddy?"

"Run."

A squeal of shock escaped her as she turned on her heel, racing off toward the stairs. Laughing, she ran up them.

"Don't run up the stairs!" he barked.

Millie rolled her eyes. He was the one who'd told her to run. What did he expect her to do?

She looked over her shoulder, thinking he'd be close behind her. After all, she wasn't a very fast runner. In fact, she didn't really like to run at all. Her boobs had a mind of their own. They were always popping out of her bra and going rogue when she attempted to run.

Frankly, it just wasn't worth it.

Unless there was a sale on dinosaurs.

Or cupcakes.

Or when your Daddy told you to run.

After all, Millie always did what she was told.

But Spike wasn't chasing after her. Instead, he just stood at the bottom of the stairs in all his glittery glory, his hands on his hips, glaring up at her.

"Watch where you're going!"

"Daddy, if you're gonna order me to run, then you can't tell me how to run!"

"Course I can. I'm your Daddy."

Hmm. Well, she couldn't really argue with that logic. When she made it to the top of the stairs safely, she heard him coming up behind her.

Thump. Thump. Thump.

Letting out another cry, her heart racing, she ran down the hallway to the bathroom.

She wasn't entirely sure why he was chasing her. Only that it was fun and exhilarating.

But where was she going to hide? She headed into the bathroom and climbed into the bath, lying down. It was the perfect hiding place.

He would never find her.

~

SHE WAS HIDING in the bath.

Millie always hid in the bath. When they were playing hide and seek. Or she'd done something naughty. Or if she just needed a few minutes to think.

She didn't even bother filling it up with water for her thinking time. She'd just lay down in it.

Apparently, it helped give her inspiration.

His girl was a nut.

And he fucking loved her.

Spike didn't know what he'd do without her. And he never intended to find out.

Sometimes he worried about losing her like he'd lost Jacqui, his first wife. She'd died during a carjacking and for a long time he'd blamed himself for not protecting her. Then Millie came along and taught him that there was more to life than existing that he'd started to forgive himself.

His girl ate up life. She lived every day like it was precious. As though she couldn't stand to waste it.

And she made him so happy.

Even when she made some sort of exploding glitter bomb and tricked him into opening it.

Spike knew he would be finding glitter in places that glitter wasn't meant to be for days.

So the Little brat was going to pay for that.

He stepped quietly into the bathroom.

Was she . . . singing to herself?

He rolled his eyes. She could at least act a bit concerned. Or like she was trying to hide.

"What are you singing?" he asked.

She screamed and put her hands over her chest, glaring up at him. "Daddy! You scared me."

He raised his eyebrows. "Did I?"

"Yes. You should apologize when you scare someone. I might have peed myself."

"Just as well you're in the bath, then. Makes it easier to clean you up."

She put her hands over her face. "I can't believe you said that."

"And I can't believe that you gave me a glitter bomb."

"Actually, it was a glitter bomb invitation." She moved her hands from her face. "Did you read it?"

"No, brat. I didn't read it. I was too busy chasing after your naughty bottom."

"Rude. Anyone would think you didn't appreciate my glitter bomb invitation."

"If that anyone is you, then yes, you should think that. I'm going to be finding glitter for days."

"Oh, yeah. You really shouldn't have run through the house like that, Daddy." She wiggled a finger at him. "You're going to have to clean that all up."

"Won't be me cleaning it up," he told her.

"Well. I don't think Mr. Fluffy will do a very good job."

"Mr. Fluffy?" he asked.

"Um, yeah. He doesn't have any thumbs. Makes it hard for him to work a vacuum or a broom."

"Right. Because that's the reason that he won't clean it up . . . his lack of thumbs."

"You really shouldn't mention that to him, though. I don't

want his feelings to be hurt. Like when the vet called him f-a-t," she whispered the last three letters.

As though she thought the damn dog could hear her.

Or spell.

Although there was no doubt that Mr. Fluffy knew the word sausage.

And diet. The look that he'd given Spike when he'd mentioned putting him on a diet . . .

Yeah, Spike had slept with one eye open that night. He shouldn't have worried, though. Mr. Fluffy was too lazy to seek revenge.

Although a few days later he found a half-eaten sausage in his boot. It had definitely felt like a threat.

"You'll be the one cleaning it all up," he told her. "Just like you're going to help clean me up."

Her mouth dropped open. "But I didn't make the mess, Daddy! You opened the invitation, and then you ran through the house, chasing me and spilling glitter. I really do think you owe me an apology."

"You know what I think I owe you?" he asked in a low voice.

She gave him a suspicious look. "No. What?"

"A spanking."

2

A spanking!

That wasn't very nice.

"I don't deserve a spanking, Daddy," she told him.

"You glitter bombed me."

"That's not a spankable offense."

"Then you laughed," he pointed out.

"Also not a spankable offense."

"It's a spankable offense if I say it's a spankable offense," he told her.

She gasped. "So you're allowed to just make rules willy-nilly now, huh, Daddy? That doesn't seem fair."

"What isn't fair, brat, is that I now have glitter in my ears. And down my T-shirt and probably in my jeans."

Huh.

She glanced at his crotch. "You need some help getting rid of that, Daddy?"

"Sure do, brat."

Reaching down, he lifted her out of the bath. He really had to stop hauling her around or he would hurt himself.

But she knew better than to say that out loud.

That *would* be a spankable offense.

Millie knew he wasn't truly serious about the spanking. Or she thought he wasn't, until he turned her around so her back was to him.

What was he doing?

"Bend down and grab hold of the edge of the bath, baby doll."

She bent over and then looked back at him. "Um, Daddy? What are you doing?"

"I told you. I'm spanking you."

"Yeah, but I didn't think you would really do it!"

"You thought wrong."

He pushed the skirt of her dress up over her bottom. She was wearing one of her favorite dresses. It was pale blue with images of dancing dinosaurs on it.

There were dinosaurs doing the mambo, dinosaurs in tutus. There was even a dinosaur in the cutest hip-hop outfit.

Now, she wished she'd worn something with more padding. Or that was harder to get access to.

"Daddy, I don't think this is very nice."

"Was it very nice to glitter bomb Daddy? And Mr. Fluffy?" he asked.

"Well, no, maybe not," she admitted. "It sure was funny, though."

Down went her panties.

Uh-oh.

Smack!

Huh. That was surprisingly light.

Smack! Smack! Smack!

He stopped and rubbed her ass.

Ohhh. So it wasn't a real spanking.

Jeez, he'd really had her convinced. Still, she felt the need to complain.

"Daddy! Ouchie!"

"Really?" he asked. "Because I could spank harder."

"No, Daddy, no! This is fine!"

"That's what I thought." Spike slid his fingers between her legs, running his fingers along her slit.

"Oh. Ohhh," she said. "That feels so good."

"Does it?" He drew his hand away to smack it down on her ass again.

And he kept going like that. He'd spank her bottom. Then he'd rub her butt cheeks before running his fingers along her slick lips.

"Please. Please," she cried out.

"Please what?" he asked.

"I need more. I need to come."

"Hmm. No, I don't think you get to come until you've apologized properly for covering me in glitter."

"I'm sorry!" she said immediately. "So sorry! So very sorry!"

"I'm not sure that's enough of an apology."

"What do you want? Me down on my knees?" she cried.

"That's exactly what I want."

OH.

Well. She could be down for that.

Literally.

"Are you laughing at a joke you told yourself?" Spike eyed her as he helped her stand.

She attempted to take her own clothes off, but he brushed her hands away and started stripping her.

"You know me well," she told him.

"Sometimes, I think I'll never know all of you. You always seem to surprise me."

She bit her lip as he helped her out of her dress. Then he reached around to undo her bra.

"Is that a bad thing?" she asked, sighing relief as her boobs were released. "Free the boobs!"

His lips twitched. "I love freeing the boobs."

Oops. She hadn't meant to say that part out loud.

"And no . . . I like your surprises. Unless you're putting yourself in danger. Those are bad surprises."

"Pfft. That hardly ever happens. I'm a good girl."

Spike's gaze ran over her. "Yeah. You're going to be a very good girl for me, aren't you?"

He slid her panties down her legs.

"Hold onto my shoulders," he said gruffly. "Lift your right foot."

She lifted her foot.

"Baby doll?"

"Yeah?" she asked, glancing down at him. Hmm, seemed he was the one on his knees now. "You know, while you're down there . . ."

"Yes?" He gave her a stern look.

"You could paint my toenails."

He snorted. "Not happening, baby."

Oh. Bummer.

"I'll do that later," he added.

Goody! For such a scary-looking guy, Spike was really just a big teddy bear.

For her, anyway.

"Also, you lifted your left foot not your right," he told her before tapping her other foot. She lifted it and he drew her panties off, throwing them behind him.

"I did? Shoot. Left and right. It's just so tricky. Does it matter, Daddy?"

"Well, it does when you're driving." He got to his feet and pulled her close, his large hands squeezing her ass.

"Good point. Probably also matters when you tell me to massage your left testicle and I massage the right."

"Have I ever asked you to massage my testicles?" He gave her an incredulous look.

"No. But I am totally here for that if that's what you need," she told him earnestly.

"I do not need."

"Good to know. I mean, these are the conversations that are important to have."

"You are so sassy."

"You like sassy, though, right?" she asked.

"Nope."

Her heart stopped.

"I love sassy." He slid his mouth over hers, kissing her. Her mouth opened under his silent demand, letting him in.

Damn.

The man could kiss.

She wrapped her arms around his neck as he lifted her, carrying her over to the shower.

Setting her down, Spike turned on the shower, then gestured to himself.

"Undress me."

Ooh, he didn't need to tell her twice.

Millie reached immediately for his belt. Undoing it.

"Not starting with my shirt, huh?"

"Nope. I like my dessert first. You know that."

A grin filled his face.

God, she loved when he smiled. He hadn't really smiled when she'd first met him. He'd been closed off and a bit grouchy.

Now, every time he smiled, it felt like a gift.

He wasn't closed off anymore.

Although he was still kind of grouchy.

After undoing his belt, she drew his jeans and boxers down his legs. As she crouched, she came face-to-face with his dick.

"Well, hello, gorgeous."

"Are you talking to my dick?" he asked.

"He's just so pretty." Leaning in, she ran her tongue over the head of his dick.

"Fuck, baby doll," he muttered. "Wait until we get in the shower."

Ooh, yes, shower blowjob.

"Left foot," she commanded as she focused on his left foot.

"Baby, that's the right foot."

"Are you sure?"

"Pretty sure."

Okay. After she got his jeans off, she stood to start on his shirt, slowly undoing each button.

God, he was so freaking sexy.

Muscular and handsome. From his bald head, down to those wide shoulders.

Millie had no idea how she was so lucky to find him.

Fate had been so freaking kind to send her to him. Part of her wondered if her sister, Daria had helped fate along. Millie hoped that she had, that Daria was watching over her.

And then to have him love her . . . that was a miracle.

She was never going to take him for granted.

After drawing off his shirt, she kissed down his chest, then his abs, moving toward her prize.

"Not yet, baby." He grabbed her arms, stopping her from going down on her knees.

"But I owe you an apology blowjob." She pouted. She didn't like having her treat taken away from her.

"You need to wash me first."

Hmm, there *was* some glitter sparkling on his face and now his chest. She glanced down and grinned.

Oh! And look! There was also some on his cock.

"It looks so festive. Maybe they should make glitter condoms or glittery cock rings. Would you wear one of those?"

"No." He opened the shower door, directing her inside before following her. "And don't even think about it."

"Sometimes, you're no fun, Daddy."

He just gave her a stern look. She grabbed his shower gel and started to lather up her hands.

"Got it lathered up enough, baby doll?" he asked dryly.

"I want to get you nice and clean," she explained as she washed his chest. She moved down his arms and then had him turn so she could do his back and ass.

Millie squeezed his butt cheeks. "Maybe you should bend over and spread."

He growled. "Not happening."

Darn it. There went that fantasy.

Oh, well.

She crouched to clean the back of his legs before he turned around. And hello!

Unable to help herself, she slid her mouth over his hard shaft.

Spike groaned. "Did I give you permission to do that?"

She moved back up his dick, letting it pop out of her mouth. "I don't need permission."

"Why is that?"

"Silly, Daddy. Because I own it."

3

Such a sassy brat.

And he loved her. Which meant she probably got away with far too much.

Bend over and spread his cheeks.

Yeah, right.

Not. Happening.

Although perhaps he should get her to do that.

Later. . .

"You own it? Pretty sure that I own you, baby doll."

Her gaze narrowed. "Are you saying that I don't own you as well?"

Yeah, Spike wasn't an idiot. He knew very well that there was only one answer to that question.

"Of course you own me as well."

"Good answer," she huffed. "Shower gel me." She held up her hand and he squirted some gel into her palm. She lathered it up before washing his legs. She started at his feet, making her way up until she reached his cock. Her hand wrapped around him, running up and down the shaft before she cupped his balls.

Fuck. Him.

This was fucking torture. Was she doing it on purpose? She was being thorough, there was no denying that. Hell, she was concentrating so hard that her tongue was sticking out of her mouth.

His breathing grew faster as he fought the urge to thrust, to order her to keep jacking him until he came.

Finally, knowing he couldn't hold back any longer, he stepped back and washed off all the suds.

Millie stayed kneeling on the floor of the shower, staring up at him.

His every dream come to life.

Curves on display. Full, heavy breasts topped with hard nipples. Silky skin. Her full mouth was slightly open as she stared up at him.

After making sure he'd washed all the soap off, Spike moved closer to her.

"Open, baby doll. Daddy is going to feed you his dick."

Her breathing seemed to grow faster at his dirty words. Liked that, did she?

"Oh. My. God. That was so dirty. I love it."

"Open," he commanded.

She parted her lips and he slid his dick into her mouth. Fuck. So. Damn. Good.

Spike pressed his cock as far as he could into her, before she started to choke, then he drew back.

"Good girl. Just relax for me. That's it." He spoke to her soothingly as the water rained down on his back and she sucked on his dick. "Tap my thigh if it gets too much."

But Millie just stared up at him with a look of such love, of such lust. And he knew she wanted this, too.

He kept his movements shallow and slow to begin with. Then he drove his cock deeper into her mouth.

God. So good.

He cupped her face as he came, his groan almost drowning out the sound of the running water.

Fuck.

"Baby, you feel so good. Drink it all down. That's my good girl. You did so well for me." He ran his thumb over her smooth cheek.

When he drew his dick out of her mouth, he was still half-hard. Leaning in, she licked him. As though she was intent on cleaning him.

Shit.

She was going to have him hard again in minutes, which he would have said was impossible.

"Baby doll. Such a good girl."

She hummed with pleasure as he wrapped her hair around his fingers.

"Come here. Let me clean you."

Reaching down, he put his hands under her arms to pick her up. Then he proceeded to wash every inch of her.

Very, very thoroughly.

By the time he rinsed her off, his dick was hard again and she was breathing heavily, her eyes filled with hunger.

With love.

Bending down, he cupped a heavy breast and sucked on her nipple.

"Ohhh. That . . . it feels like you're sucking on my clit when you do that," she said breathlessly.

"Yeah? What about when I do this?" He flicked her nipple with his tongue.

"God. So good," she moaned. "More, I need more."

"Not sure that girls who glitter bomb their Daddy, then get their butt smacked, deserve more."

"Daddy, we're the ones who *do* deserve more," she told him earnestly.

He snorted.

"Please. I really, really need to come." She put her hands together in front of her chest, begging him. "I think I might injure something if I don't get to come."

He raised his eyebrows. "Injure something? Like this?" He ran his finger lightly over her clit. She threw her head back. She was flushed from the heat of the shower, her hair wet, her skin damp.

Fucking beautiful.

"Yes. More. Harder."

"No. You don't make demands. You get what you're given."

She whimpered, biting down on her lip. He wasn't having that. Leaning in, he kissed her, sliding his tongue over her abused lip when she immediately let go.

"Open. Let me in." He pressed his mouth to hers again and she immediately parted her lips.

He loved it when she did as he ordered.

He continued his soft, slow movement over her clit, swallowing her whimpers of protest. Swapping to his thumb, he pushed two fingers deep inside her.

"Please. Please," she begged when he drew back from her kiss.

"Turn around and then bend over."

Her eyes widened with a mix of trepidation and excitement.

"And spread."

Her breathing increased. His girl loved ass play.

And he loved to indulge her.

Win-win.

Turning around, she bent over.

"Spread them, baby," he murmured. He wrapped his hand around the base of his dick, squeezing hard.

Christ.

He thought he could come again just from watching her part her ass cheeks for him.

Thankfully, he kept some silicone-based lube in the shower for just this reason. Grabbing it, he coated two of his fingers and then ran them over her back hole.

"Ohh," she moaned.

"Easy, baby," he told her. Slowly, he slid one finger inside her.

"More. More!" she cried, trying to push back on his finger.

Slap!

He smacked her ass cheek.

"Naughty girls don't get to come. They get their ass finger-fucked and then they're made to go to bed without any orgasms."

"Noooo," she cried. "I'll be good. I'll be good."

Yeah. Somehow, he doubted that.

Not that he minded.

"Let go of your ass," he told her. "Drop your hands."

She did as she was told.

"Such a good girl."

"Does that mean I get to come, Daddy?" she asked.

"Perhaps. Step back and then put your hands on the wall of the shower. Good. Spread your legs."

Fuck, yes. She was bent over in front of him, his fingers still buried deep in her ass.

Reaching around, he rubbed lightly at her clit as he drove his fingers in and out of her bottom.

"Oh. Ohhh. Please."

"Not yet," he told her. "You're not to come yet."

A whimper escaped her. He wondered if she'd manage to hold her orgasm back. She was so slick. Ready for him.

"That's it. Such a good girl." He slid his fingers from her ass and quickly washed them before grabbing her hips.

He started to press his dick into her. Inch by inch.

Nice and slow.

Fuck. Her pussy was clenching around him, pulling him in.

"Baby, you have no idea how good you feel," he murmured.

"I have some idea," she told him breathlessly. "You feel so amazing inside me."

He placed his hands on the shower wall above hers. Then he fucked her with shallow, hard thrusts.

So. Good.

"More. I need more," she cried.

"You're going to come like this."

"I can't." She shook her head. "I can't."

"Then reach down and play with yourself. Because you're coming when I do. Or you don't get to come at all."

How DID she get such a mean Daddy?

She didn't get to come unless she came with him?

And she had to touch herself?

All right. She could do this. She had to come. She was desperate. Reaching one hand down, she rubbed her clit.

Ohhh. That felt so good.

"Wait for me, baby doll," he warned.

She couldn't. There was no way. Millie bit down on her lip, slowing her movements. Her breath sawed in and out of her lungs.

"I'm close, baby," Spike told her. "Come on my cock."

Moving her finger faster, it seemed that was all she needed.

He commanded. She obeyed.

Well, some of the time.

Her orgasm hit her hard, making her shake as she heard him groan. He thrust deep and stilled, then drew her up so she was standing with her back pressed against his chest.

"Baby."

That was all he said.

But really, he didn't need to say more.

She understood him.

4

Millie felt that familiar wave of nausea rush through her.

She swallowed heavily, trying to convince herself that she wasn't going to throw up.

She didn't have time for a migraine right now.

The side of her face was tingling as her vision grew blurry. Meds. She needed her meds.

Were they upstairs?

Holy. Crap.

Why couldn't she think?

Heaving herself off the sofa, she whimpered as a sharp pain sliced through her head. She'd been finishing off the invitations to her super-duper amazing Easter egg hunt.

This time without the glitter.

Because Spike was a total killjoy.

She'd intended to send them all out today. Spike was going to take them to Reapers to give to the guys and she'd been going to deliver one to Grady, Steele, and Effie.

Although she hadn't told Spike that part.

She stumbled toward the stairs. Her migraine was coming on fast. Maybe she'd been pushing herself too hard with this Easter egg hunt?

Nah. That was foolish talk.

"Think, Millie," she muttered to herself.

Oh God.

She was going to vomit. She rushed toward the downstairs bathroom, but didn't make it in time. Instead, she sank to her knees in the hallway and vomited.

Yucky.

Shuffling away from the vomit, she lay down on her side and put her arms over her face, trying to block out the light.

Spike wasn't going to be very happy when he got home. He hated when she got migraines.

She heard a low whine and glanced over to see a blurry-looking Mr. Fluffy standing beside her. He had her handbag in his mouth.

Why would he have my handbag? And did he really walk here all the way from the living room? Voluntarily?

Now that was a miracle.

Too bad he didn't some thumbs so he could call Spike for her.

She really, really wanted her Daddy.

SPIKE WALKED INTO THE HOUSE.

Instantly, he knew something was wrong. The house was just too quiet.

Which was very unlike Millie. There was always music or chatter or laughter. Even when she was by herself. Because she was usually talking away to the dog as though she thought he could understand her.

Hell, most of the time, Mr. Fluffy wasn't even awake. Spike had never known a living creature to sleep that much.

The vet had done all types of tests on him.

And the diagnosis?

An extreme version of laziness.

"Millie?" he called out in a panic. "Millie, where are you?"

A whine reached his ears.

"Mr. Fluffy?"

Another whine. Fuck. Spike ran toward the sound, coming to a stop as he saw Millie lying on her side in the hallway. There was vomit on the floor next to her and Mr. Fluffy was lying on his tummy, watching her.

Strangely, her handbag was by the dog's feet.

"Shit, baby doll," he murmured, coming closer and crouching next to her.

With a shaking hand, he reached out to touch her. She let out a small whimper.

"Daddy," she whispered.

"Baby, what is it? Your head?"

"Yes."

Shit. She needed her medication.

Mr. Fluffy let out another whine and nudged her handbag.

What the . . . then it struck him.

Had Mr. Fluffy gotten her handbag because he knew that her meds were in there?

Had he somehow realized that she had a migraine?

Nah. That was just crazy thinking. Although as Spike looked into the dog's eyes . . . he kind of thought that maybe it wasn't so crazy.

"I'm going to pick you up, baby doll, and carry you upstairs."

"Can't. Move."

"We have to move you. You can't stay here."

"Sick."

"I know you are."

"Sorry."

Why was she apologizing? This wasn't her fault.

She couldn't help having a migraine. If anything, this was his fault.

He should have been here. Should have been watching her. Making sure that she rested and didn't do too much.

Shit . . . it was probably all this excitement over her party.

"You have nothing to apologize for, baby doll," he told her fiercely. "Daddy is going to pick you up, though. And carry you upstairs."

Another whimper.

God. He felt awful for her. If he could've taken this pain on, he would have. Sliding his arm under her legs and around her back, Spike lifted her up, cradling her against his chest.

Another cry that nearly broke his heart.

Trying hard not to jostle her, he headed up the stairs and into their bedroom, where he laid her on the bed. Then he rushed into the attached bathroom to grab her medication. She kept some up here and some in her handbag.

When he returned, he wasn't surprised to see Mr. Fluffy sitting beside the bed, his head on the mattress as he stared at Millie. The only time the dog showed any signs of life was when Millie was in pain. The rest of the time, he was a lazy ball of fur.

Although he'd never known the dog to grab her handbag. Maybe he hadn't. Perhaps Millie had picked it up, then collapsed before she could get her medication out.

"Baby doll, pills." He sat on the bed, facing her. There was already a bottle of water on the nightstand.

"Noo," she moaned as he drew her carefully up with his hand behind her head, supporting her.

"Yes," he replied firmly. "You need these pills."

"Noo."

"Millie, do as Daddy says. Open your mouth."

To his surprise, she actually parted her lips and he put the pills on her tongue, then helped her take a few sips of water.

"That's Daddy's good girl." He laid her back down and then grabbed a blanket to place over her, tucking it around her.

Then he pulled all the curtains closed. Darkness and quiet was what she needed right now.

Closing the door to the hallway, he drew a chair over to the bed and sat on it, taking her wrist in his hand. He placed his fingers on her pulse.

Steady pulse.

Logically, he knew it was a migraine and that she would be all right. But he didn't always operate on logic when it came to his girl. He had to make certain that she was well. That's why he sometimes sat there, watching her breathe, monitoring her pulse.

Just to make sure that she was still with him.

Because she wasn't ever allowed to leave him.

Spike wasn't sure he could ever live without Millie.

"I'm okay," she said in a pained voice. "Sorry I worried you."

"Shh," he told her. "You don't need to worry about me. You need to be sleeping."

"Love you."

"I love you too, baby doll. Rest now. Daddy is here to take care of you."

5

Millie felt like crap.

Pure and utter crap.

Opening her eyes, she stared straight into Mr. Fluffy's face.

"Your breath stinks."

"Woof."

Awesome. Just what she needed. Some more air in her face.

"Still stinks," she muttered.

He just gave her a huff of disbelief and then drew away, flopping down with a groan.

Right. She got the message. She was hard work.

With a moan, she sat up. The world kind of swum for a moment and she had to convince her stomach that she didn't need to vomit up its meager contents.

It was a hard fight, though.

She hated the aftermath of a migraine almost as much as she detested the migraine itself. She always felt like a train had run her over, then backed up to run over her again.

But as much as she just wanted to hide in bed and forget any of this had happened, she really, really needed to pee.

She stood and the world spun again.

"Stupid building. Stay still," she muttered.

Mr. Fluffy let out another bark. She wasn't sure what he was trying to say. It was difficult to tell the difference between 'stupid human' and 'I love you.' She kind of thought it might be something in the middle.

Moving forward, she stumbled her way to the bathroom and collapsed on the toilet with a sigh.

Then she nearly cried as she realized she still had panties on.

"Stupid panties."

"I don't know, I'm rather fond of your panties," Spike told her quietly.

She could have cried in relief. "Daddy. Panties."

"Yes, I know. You think they're stupid."

"Off." Millie didn't care that she was sitting on the toilet. That she was basically asking him to strip her off.

She had to pee.

Right. Freaking. Now.

"Millie," Spike grumbled. "Why didn't you call for me?" He lifted her to her feet and reached under her skirt to pull her panties down before sitting her back on the toilet.

A sigh of relief left her as she peed. "Didn't know where you were."

"I had the baby monitor on. I would have heard you."

Okay. She made a mental note to complain about him watching her sleep later. When she had energy. Right now, she barely had the energy to clean herself up.

Lifting her, Spike carried her back into the bedroom and laid her on the bed.

"I don't wanna go back to bed, Daddy."

He eyed her, then grunted. She wasn't sure if that was a grunt of agreement or not.

Sometimes she was well-versed in Spike-Speak. Other times, not so much. But he picked her back up, cradling her against him like she was tiny.

When she definitely wasn't.

But Spike made her feel that way. Like she was fragile and precious.

He walked into her playroom. She loved her playroom. The cream walls with decals all over them. The huge tree that spanned almost two full walls with little fairy houses hanging from the branches. Along with fairies flying through the air.

Then there was her karaoke machine and stage as well as her reading corner.

She loved her playroom.

Spike laid her down on the bed, then gave her Chompers.

"Chompers! Where did you come from?" she asked.

"Just appeared out of thin air," Spike told her.

She sighed and hugged her toy dinosaur tight. "Always knew you was magic. You know any fairies?"

"I know lots of fairies, magnificent, marvelous Millie," she replied in Chompers voice.

"Magnificent, marvelous Millie, huh?" Spike asked.

"That's my name, Daddy. You should start using it," she replied tiredly.

Spike snorted as he walked over to the closet, returning with a dinosaur onesie. This onesie even had a hood with a dinosaur face on it.

Millie didn't even try to help as he undressed her. He gave her a worried look, but she smiled up at him.

"Just tired, Daddy."

"Okay, baby doll. Your job today is just to rest, then. Let Daddy take care of you."

"Daddy always takes good care of Millie the Magnificent," she replied.

"Are you just trying out names to see what you like best?" he asked as he finished putting the onesie on her.

"Uh-huh."

"My vote is the second one," he told her.

"Has a nice ring to it," she agreed as she attempted to sit up.

"Uh-uh." He placed a hand gently, but firmly on her chest. "Thought we agreed that Daddy is taking care of you today."

"I can'ts sit up?"

"Nope."

Huh. Okay. She didn't have the energy to argue. And why would she want to?

"I'm going to put you in your pod while I get you some food and a bottle, all right?"

She wrinkled her nose. "No food."

"Yes, food."

"No bottle."

Spike gave her a firm look, his hands on his hips. "Are you just arguing for the sake of it?"

"I wouldn't do that, Daddy. Millie the Miraculous doesn't be naughty."

"That one wasn't as good," he told her.

"Yeah, I could sense it sucked."

Lifting her, he placed her in her pod. Well, that's what they called it. It was this large round seat that sort of sucked you into it. It was green and the back of it had a dinosaur head on the top of it.

When she sat in it, it surrounded her, supporting her.

Also, she couldn't really get out of it on her own. Not without a lot of huffing and puffing and a fair amount of humiliation thrown in.

Spike made sure she had Chompers, then he grabbed her dinosaur pacifier. She opened her mouth and he popped it in.

"Stay."

Millie wrinkled her nose. How rude. She was not a dog. She was a dinosaur-fairy-loving Little.

Stay. Pfft.

Although to be fair, she did stay. He returned shortly after with a sandwich and a bottle with some pink water in it.

Fairy juice! Yes!

Daddy was so good to her. Spike placed the plate and bottle down, then sat in front of her.

He drew the pacifier from her mouth.

"Fairy juice! Yummy!"

"You have to eat some food first," he told her sternly.

"No food." She pouted.

"Millie the Naughty is going to do as she is told," Spike warned.

"Um, Daddy, that isn't right. You need to use M words."

"Couldn't think of one," he muttered.

"Yeah, it's tough when you aren't as magnificent as me," she agreed. "Maybe one day you'll be this good, Daddy. If you practice."

"One can only hope," he agreed solemnly.

Indeed. One could.

"You're still eating your sandwich first," he said sternly. "Cheese and mayo."

Millie let out a long-suffering sigh. "Fine. If I must."

He held a piece up to her mouth and she took a bite, chewing slowly. After a few bites, she had to admit that she felt a bit better. The nausea in her stomach eased and a small surge of energy filled her.

But she wouldn't tell him that. You should never tell a Daddy that he was right. It set a bad precedent.

Then he'd start to think that he was always right. And that just wasn't a good idea for a Little. Not if they wanted to save their bottoms.

When the sandwich was gone, Spike held up the bottle for her. Millie grabbed hold, drinking down some fairy juice.

She could feel the magic already. Spike disappeared with the plate and when he returned he had her medicine.

Removing the bottle from her mouth, she took the pills without protesting.

"Good girl," he praised her.

Well, of course she was. She was always a good girl.

"What would you like to do? It should be something quiet and restful."

Pfft. Sounded boring.

"I feels loads better, Daddy. I think I might build an Easter egg. For the Easter Bunny. Or maybe make a welcome sign."

He raised his eyebrows. "And how were you going to build this sign?"

"With Lego, of course, Daddy." She gave him a look that told him he was silly. "How else?"

"Of course. What was I thinking?"

She didn't know. He was a Daddy. Who knew how they thought?

If she could figure that out . . . imagine how much naughtiness she'd get away with.

Heck. She could write a book. How to be naughty and not get your butt spanked: The key to controlling your Daddy.

She'd sell so many. Then she could go on tour. Take over the world . . . the possibilities were endless.

HMM.

Spike wondered what Millie was thinking. That was definitely her, 'I'm going to conquer the world' look.

Lord knew if he didn't keep a close eye on her, he was pretty sure she could take over the world.

And then it would be cake for breakfast, ice cream for lunch, and fairy juice for dinner.

"I'll get your Lego for you," he told her.

Best to keep her distracted when she got that look on her face.

Grabbing the tub that held her Lego, he put it on the rug as she attempted to get out of her dinosaur pod. He loved that pod. It was one of the few ways he had to keep her contained.

The door to the playroom opened and Mr. Fluffy wandered in, flopping down on his side about a foot into the room as if he couldn't possibly make it to his dog bed.

Spike just shook his head at him as he lifted Millie out of the pod and set her on the mat. He'd keep a close eye on her to make certain that she wasn't overdoing it. She tended to ignore how she was feeling when she was busy.

That's why she needed him.

"What do you think, Daddy? Do you think the Easter Bunny will like my creation?"

"I think he'll love it, baby doll."

She frowned, staring it over. Then she shook her head, wincing as she did.

"It's not big enough, it needs to be grander. Something that will wow him. I want the Easter Bunny to leave lots of chocolate for me and my friends. What if he comes here and thinks that the sign is crappy and not big enough and then leaves?"

"Baby, that's not going to happen," he soothed.

"It might! You don't know, Daddy! I wants this to be perfect for all my friends."

Shit. She was getting wound up. He knew it was because she

was still feeling tired and out-of-sorts. But this wasn't going to help her feel any better.

"That's enough playing for today. It's nearly dinnertime."

"No, Daddy! I have to get it right." Millie gave him a stubborn look.

He cupped her chin in his hand. "No, what you need to do is listen to Daddy. We'll put your creation away somewhere safe, then pack this up. Dinner and an early night."

"No, Daddy! No dinner and an early night. Leave my Lego alone."

"Millie," he said warningly. "I'm going to give you one more chance to pack up your Lego like a good girl."

"And if I don't?" she challenged.

"Then you're spending some time in the corner." He wouldn't spank her when she'd just had a migraine. No way did he want to risk hurting her. But corner time was definitely a punishment she could handle.

Her lower lip trembled and he had to harden himself against giving in and letting her do whatever she wanted.

Spike knew her tricks.

"You're being so mean, Daddy. All I was trying to do was make something beautiful for the Easter Bunny."

"And you have," he said. "But now it's time to pack up." He scooped up a handful of Lego pieces and put them in the tub. With a sigh, Millie started to help. Then he lifted her creation and set it on the shelves.

"I still don't think it's good enough."

"You're too hard on yourself." When all of the Lego was put away, he grabbed Chompers and gave him to her. Picking up her pacifier, he placed it in her mouth. Then he scooped her up onto his hip and carried her out of the room.

Mr. Fluffy let out a woof of protest as they went past.

"If you want fed, dog, you're going to need to get yourself down the stairs."

Millie pulled the pacifier from her mouth. "That's not kind, Daddy. I think we need to put in an elevator."

"We're not putting in an elevator for him."

"What about one of them dumb waiter thingees?" she asked. "He could ride in that."

"Nope."

"How about a sled that he can ride down the stairs and then attach a pulley system to get him back up?"

"Also nope."

Millie sighed. "Don't you love Mr. Fluffy, Daddy?"

"I like him. But I'm not hauling his heavy ass up the stairs on a sled. And he needs the exercise."

"That is true, Mr. Fluffy," she called back. "You do need the exercise! The vet said so."

There was a growling noise from her playroom.

"Oh, I said the V-E-T word," Millie whispered. "Oops."

Spike started down the stairs.

"Be careful, Daddy. Don't slip."

"I won't slip. Precious cargo."

"You're the best Daddy ever."

"Only because I've got the best girl in the world."

6

S pike set her down in her special high chair at the table. He strapped her in before placing some toys on the tray for her to play with.

"It's dinosaur feeding time!" she cried as her dinosaurs started to battle it out.

After putting some pasta on to boil, he sat at the table and grabbed his phone.

"Who you texting, Daddy?" she asked suspiciously. "It's not the Easter Bunny, is it? You're not telling him not to come, are you?"

"Why would I do that?" Spike asked, looking surprised.

"Because I was a bad girl and didn't listen to you. I won't do it anymore, Daddy. I will be a good girl. I promise."

"Hey." Standing, he around the table so he was in front of her. Bending down, he grasped her chin in his hand, tilting her face up. "You could never do anything that would make me tell the Easter Bunny or Santa or anyone else not to come, understand? You're a good girl."

"Promise?"

"I promise." Leaning forward, he kissed her forehead, then her nose. "I'm just texting Reyes to let him know I won't be into Reapers tonight. We're having a vote on whether to let Stone become a member."

"But you have to go tonight, Daddy!" she said in alarm as he set the phone down and went back to cooking dinner.

"What? Why?" he asked.

"Because you need to deliver the invitations."

"Baby doll, I'm not leaving you after a migraine like that. I'll deliver them another day."

"Tomorrow?"

He eyed her. "We'll see."

Oh no. She didn't like the sound of 'we'll see.'

"They have to be delivered tomorrow, Daddy," she told him as he moved back to the stove to drain the pasta. "Please?"

"All right. Daddy will deliver them tomorrow."

Millie clapped her hands. "You're the best Daddy ever!"

"Is that because you think you have Daddy wrapped around your little finger?" he asked dryly as he put a plate of pasta in front of her. He sat on the chair facing her and forked some up.

"Daddy, I never thought that." She gave him a shocked look.

That was a lie.

A little white one.

Because she totally thought that.

Spike fed her a bite of the pasta and she ate it slowly. Yummy. He knew just how to make it the way she liked.

Cheesy and delicious.

"Are you not eating, Daddy?" she asked in concern.

"I'll eat soon, baby doll. Gonna get you fed and settled, then Daddy will eat. My baby comes first."

Yep. Best Daddy ever.

"Daddy, I can feeds myself," she told him proudly. "Then you can eats."

"I like feeding you, though."

She smiled at him and he fed her several more bites until she shook her head. "Enough, Daddy."

He got up with the plate and put it in the dishwasher before returning with one of her sippy cups filled with water.

"Can I have fairy juice?" she asked, wrinkling her nose at the cup of plain water.

"No more fairy juice. Just plain water."

Millie sighed. "That sucks."

Spike just gave her a look as he stood there.

"I mean, thanks, Daddy!"

"Yep. That's what I thought you meant to say."

Silly Daddy. Well, she'd let him have his delusions while she drank boring water.

Picking up the sippy cup, she gulped it down with a big sigh of satisfaction.

"Good?" Spike asked.

"Yep. That's the good stuff, Daddy."

He snorted in amusement. She shuffled around on her seat. "Daddy, down!"

"Excuse me?" he asked in a low voice.

"Daddy, down!"

What was so hard to understand about that?

Spike put his hands on his hips as he gave her a stern look. "Is that how we ask for something?"

"Umm." She was sensing that it was not.

"Someone has forgotten their manners." After grabbing some wet wipes from the table, he tilted her face back so he could wash it. Next, he wiped her fingers and hands. "I think that someone needs some corner time so that they can make better choices."

"Is that someone Chompers? Because I think he ate a chocolate bar for breakfast." She glanced down at Chompers who sat beside her on the high-chair. "Make better choices, Chompers."

"Chompers isn't the one who is going into timeout. That would be Millie."

She gasped. "Me, Daddy?"

"You." He undid her straps, then lifted off the tray.

That's when Millie thought she'd make her move. If she could just get away from him, then she could run . . . run like the wind!

Of course, she conveniently forgot that she hated to run.

And, as usual, Spike was one step ahead of her. He caught her as she tried to slide off the seat.

"What do you think you are doing?" he asked.

"Um, getting down, Daddy."

"Are you allowed to get down on your own?" he asked.

"I can do it, Daddy."

"That's not what I asked, Millie."

Shoot.

"No, Daddy."

"No, because you could hurt yourself. Were you planning on running from me?"

She gasped. "You know I don't like to run."

"You don't mind running when it saves you from a timeout. Or a hot butt."

"No one said anything about a hot butt, Daddy!"

"Well, someone might need one."

"That seems a bit harsh. Poor Chompers was just doing what a dinosaur does."

Spike grunted, then lifted her into the air, putting her on his hip. He carried her into the living room and set her down by the corner.

"Stay there. I'll get you a chair."

"I don't need a chair, Daddy."

"You just had a migraine, you're not standing."

That wasn't exactly what she'd meant.

"I mean I don't need a chair because I don't need to spend any time in the corner. I'm already sorry for forgetting my manners. I just lost my head for a moment. It happens to the best of us."

"I can see that," he agreed. "Lucky for you, you have a Daddy to help you remember these things. Stay."

Darn it.

Why could she never talk him out of these punishments? It's like he thought he was doing it for her own good or something.

Silly Daddy.

He returned with a chair from the dining table and set it down in front of her, facing the corner.

"Turn around and sit."

Millie thought about protesting. But she really didn't want a sore bottom.

So, with a huff, she did as ordered.

"Good girl. Now, you're going to sit there for ten minutes and think about what you did and what you could have done differently. Understand?"

"Yes, Daddy. I will."

She was nothing if not obedient.

"Give me Chompers." He held out his hand for her toy dinosaur.

"I don't know, Daddy. Chompers has been rather naughty today. Chocolate bar for breakfast, remember? I think it might do him some good to contemplate his circumstances."

"Hmm. You could be right."

"I am right." Millie was always right.

She hated corner time. Of course, she didn't think anyone

really ever liked it. But it sucked sitting here, doing nothing. Sure, she was meant to be contemplating her circumstances. But that didn't sound like much fun, if you asked her.

"All right, baby doll. You can come out of the corner now."

Oh, thank goodness.

Standing, the room kind of spun and she had to sit down abruptly. Mr. Fluffy let out an alarmed bark as Chompers slid to the floor.

Spike rushed over to pick her up, holding her against his chest. "Hey, are you all right?"

"Me? Yep. I'm good, Daddy. Everything just spun for a moment."

"Shit. Fuck. Shouldn't have put you in the corner." He lifted her up against his chest and carried her to the sofa, laying her down on her back. A cushion was placed under her head and then several more were put under her calves to raise her feet up in the air.

"Daddy, I'm okay."

"You nearly fainted."

"I didn't nearly faint," she countered. "I just got the spins. I probably stood up too fast."

There was guilt in his face as stared down at her. "Maybe I should call Hack. Yeah, that's what I'll do."

Shoot. He looked so worried.

Reaching up, she grasped hold of his hand. "I'm fine, Daddy. I promise. I don't need Hack. I just stood up too fast. You know the effects of a migraine can last for a while."

"Yeah, that's true. But that means I shouldn't have put you in timeout."

"Daddy," she scolded. "I'm fine. I deserved it. I promise I'm okay."

He cupped the side of her face, staring down at her. "All

right. But from now on, I'll help you up. And you're taking it easy. Early night for you."

"Okay, Daddy. I love you."

He crouched before leaning forward to kiss her lightly. "Love you too, baby doll."

7

Millie buzzed around the backyard. Everyone was arriving in a few hours for the Super-Duper Easter Egg hunt and she was so excited. She stood still and looked around all of the trees. She'd set up two tables. Well, Spike had put out the tables but she'd done all the decorating. One table had a pink tablecloth with lots of cane baskets on top.

Those were for all her Little friends to collect the eggs that the Easter Bunny was going to put out. That reminded her . . . she needed to make sure that Spike knew where his costume was. Couldn't have an Easter Bunny who didn't look like a bunny.

"That would just be silly, Mr. Fluffy."

Mr. Fluffy gave her a long-suffering look. He'd already gotten dressed.

"You look so adorable, Mr. Fluffy. Look at you. So cute." He had a set of Easter Bunny ears on his head and he wore a fluffy white coat that had a rabbit tail resting just above his own tail.

"You can be the Easter Bunny's helper," she told him. "But no eating any chocolate. It's not good for you."

"Woof."

Good. He understood.

She glanced over at the other table which was filled with Easter treats. There were cupcakes with bunny faces, cinnamon rolls in the shapes of bunnies, chocolate nests with small eggs in them. Oh and some sandwiches because Daddy had told her that there needed to be something healthy on the plate.

Pfft. Sometimes she didn't think that Daddy fully understood Easter. He had to get into the Easter spirit.

Think big or go home.

There was also a drinks dispenser filled with pink fairy juice and some cute cups with more Easter eggs on them.

Yep. Everything looked amazing.

Including her, if she did say so herself.

She had on a pale blue dress with Easter eggs stitched along the hem. A pink belt cinched it around her waist. And she'd made her own Easter-themed headband. It had flowers with a little rabbit peeking out. She'd made one for each of her friends too. They were in their baskets.

After being shot, she wasn't sure that she'd be able to make her own clothes and accessories again. But Spike had hired the best people he could find to help with her rehabilitation. While she had to be careful not to push herself too hard, she was so grateful that she could still create things.

"Baby doll."

Turning, she smiled at Spike. "Well, Daddy? What do you think? Doesn't it look awesome? Or should that be eggsome?"

He glanced around. "You've done a great job, baby."

She smiled with delight. "Thanks, Daddy! Are you ready to go pick up Reverend Pat and the others?" She'd finally convinced her friends from Nowhere to start flying here instead of driving all the way. And they'd actually listened this time.

Probably due to the fact that Andrey was the only one who hadn't lost his license yet and no one trusted him to stay on the right side of the road. Or use his brakes.

Reverend Pat had been driving a few months ago and had run off the road. Millie had been terrified after she'd found out that he'd passed out at the wheel. He was all right now, but he was on medication to help with his heart. She still worried about him and the others. They were all getting older and she lived so far away from them.

However, she knew that she could visit whenever she liked and that they were being looked after.

She just hated to think of the day that something might happen to them.

Don't think about it right now.

Appreciate them while you have them.

"Yep."

"And you'll come straight back? Don't let Mr. Spain talk you into going to the lawnmower shop again."

That had happened once when Spike was meant to be taking them to the grocery store. They'd been gone for four hours, and by the time they got home, Spike had been the one with the migraine.

Who knew there was so much to look at in a lawnmower store?

"We're coming straight here. Trust me," Spike said grimly.

"Goody! I'm so excited! Everyone will be here in about three hours. Okay?"

"Which means you have time for a rest," Spike said firmly.

"What? No. I don't need to rest."

"Yes, you do. Or you're gonna get too excited and run out of energy before anyone even gets here."

"That won't happen, Daddy! And I've got too much to do!"

Spike raised his eyebrows, glancing around. "Like what?"

"Um, well, I've got to . . . um . . . I have to . . . well . . . I don't know."

"Right. Which means that you can come and lie down while I go and get your friends. Come on." He took hold of her hand and led her inside, then up the stairs.

"Daddy, I really think that a nap will be detrimental to my hunting abilities."

"Your hunting abilities," he repeated slowly.

"Uh-huh."

"What are you hunting?" he asked as he reached her playroom.

"Eggs, of course. Daddy, have you already forgotten what today is?" She shook her head slowly. "Poor Daddy, losing his memory."

"I haven't forgotten what today is. I didn't realize you needed hunting abilities to find Easter eggs."

"Um, then why would it be called an Easter egg hunt if you didn't have to hunt?"

Silly Daddy.

"Yes. I suppose you're right."

"I usually am, Daddy," she replied as he had her sit on the bed so he could crouch in front of her to remove her shoes.

"How is a nap going to be detrimental to your hunting abilities?" he asked.

"It's quite simple, Daddy. Because it will make me all sluggish and sleepy and then I won't be able to run as fast or sniff out those eggs. Now do you understand?"

"I do. But I can tell you that your nap won't hold you back."

He helped her lay down on her bed and pulled a blanket over her.

She yawned as he handed her Chompers. "How do you know, Daddy?"

"Because you won't be running around. You'll be walking. And then you won't miss any eggs. Will you?"

"That sounds like Daddy logic." She eyed him suspiciously.

"Well, I am a Daddy."

"Yeah, you're a tricky one." She waggled a finger at him. "I'm watching you."

Spike picked up her pacifier and placed it in her mouth. "I'll be back soon. Take a nap like a good girl."

Pfft. Millie was always a good girl.

WHERE THE HECK WAS SPIKE?

Worry filled her as she checked her watch. People were due to arrive in just less than an hour and Spike wasn't here yet. Nor were several of her special guests.

Shoot. She should have insisted that they fly into Billings yesterday. But Reverend Pat had wanted to attend the Easter Sunday service in Nowhere. He was no longer an active minister, but he still liked to help the new minister with his duties.

And by 'help' she meant that he liked to lecture him on the correct way to do things.

That's why she'd decided to have her hunt on Monday instead of Easter Sunday. Her friends were staying for a whole week, much to Spike and Mr. Fluffy's horror.

But they'd deal. For her, there wasn't much they wouldn't do.

Millie checked her phone again to see if there had been a delay in the flight coming in. But no, it said it landed forty minutes ago which should have given him plenty of time to get here.

Although she knew that getting her friends to do something was like herding cats. So perhaps Spike was just having trouble getting them all into his car.

Yep. That was it. That's all that was wrong.

Nothing else.

It couldn't be anything else.

They might have gone to the lawnmower store again. Mr. Spain could be awfully persuasive.

Except . . . why wasn't Spike answering his phone?

A sob escaped her. Maybe he couldn't hear it over Andrey's loud voice. Or everyone having to yell at Mr. Spain because he couldn't hear them.

God, she hoped so.

A ping on her phone told her someone was at the gate. Hope flooded her before she realized that Spike would just drive in.

She frowned as she saw a strange car at the gates. Spike would kill her if she let someone in who she didn't know. It was a large car. Was it someone coming early to the hunt? But most people knew the code.

Then her gaze zeroed in on the person in the front passenger seat.

Was that . . . was it . . . Andrey?

But why would he be in a strange car?

The passenger door opened and Andrey stepped out. She immediately opened the gate remotely. What was going on?

Why wasn't Spike driving them? Where was he?

A knot developed in her stomach and she rang Spike's phone again as she made her way around to the front of the house.

It went to voicemail.

Where are you, Daddy?

The car had stopped and a stranger was opening the trunk.

"Hello!" she called out.

"Ahh, Millie!" Andrey cried, opening his arms wide. "We are here! Safe and sound."

"Safe, yes," Reverend Pat muttered as he climbed out of the back, then turned to help Mrs. Larsen.

Mr. and Mrs. Spain got out from the other side.

"But some of us are not so sound," Reverend Pat added.

"Ahh, old man." Andrey whacked Reverend Pat on his back. "Do not be so hard on yourself. Not all of us can be as good up here as me." He tapped his head.

"That's not what I meant," Reverend Pat said. "You tried to get us here by hitchhiking."

"What? What is wrong with that?" Andrey asked.

"Guys," she said, trying to catch their attention. They could do this for hours if she let them.

And she needed to know what had happened.

"It's dangerous," Reverend Pat said, his face growing red. "We could have been killed."

"Pfft," Andrey said. "As if I would allow that to happen. I could kill this man forty ways with my bare hands. No problem."

The driver paled.

"Wait. You hitchhiked here?" she asked.

That feeling of dread in her tummy grew.

Where. Was. Spike?

"No, we did not," Reverend Pat said as the man finished emptying his trunk. "We got an Uber."

"You guys know how to Uber?" she asked, temporarily distracted from her worries.

"Of course we know how to use Uber," Mrs. Larsen said with a huff.

"So he's an Uber driver." She gestured to the man who was getting back into his car now that everyone was out.

"Yes, of course," Reverend Pat said.

"We thought that Spike was picking us up," Mrs. Spain said. "When he didn't turn up, we decided that we better get our own way here."

"You . . . what? He didn't turn up?" Millie was going to pass out. She couldn't . . . couldn't . . .

"Millie? Millie!" Someone caught her, lowering her to the ground. She looked up into the concerned face of Reverend Pat, then behind to Andrey who'd caught her.

"Where . . . where is Spike?" she asked, her panic growing.

What happened? Something bad . . . she knew it had to be something bad. Or he'd have been at the airport. He'd be answering his phone.

Her phone started ringing.

Was it Spike?

"Where . . . where's my phone? It's ringing. It might be Spike."

"It's in your hand, dear," Mrs. Spain said.

She stared down at her phone, but for some reason she couldn't seem to make herself answer it.

Millie tried to clear her vision. To make herself read what was written on the screen. But it had gone all blurry.

All she knew was that it wasn't Spike's ringtone.

His current ringtone was one she'd found called Big Bad Daddy. It was hilarious.

Answer the phone, Millie.

What if . . . what if something had happened to him? And answering this call made it real?

A sob broke free. Suddenly, her phone was pulled from her tight grasp. She glanced up through blurry eyes at Reverend Pat as he answered the call.

"Yes? No, she's indisposed at the moment, who is this? Yes . . . yes . . . I'm her . . . father."

Another sob.

"I will tell her. We'll be there soon. Thank you."

"What's happened?" she asked as tears dripped down her cheeks.

He hesitated.

"Please," she begged. She'd gone from not wanting to know to needing to. "Just tell me."

"It's Spike. There's been an accident and we need to get to the hospital."

Oh. God.

8

---

*H*old it together. Hold it together.

But she couldn't. She really couldn't.

Millie paced up and down the waiting room. What was going on? Where was Spike?

A sob escaped her and she wiped at her cheeks.

"Millie?"

She glanced over to see Damon stepping into the waiting room, his face pale and worried.

She ran at him and he caught her, his arm under her ass as he lifted her into his arms and held her cradled against his chest.

"It's all right. You're okay."

"I'm not. I'm not. Spike . . ." His name was a cry on her lips. Filled with pain and fear.

"Do we know anything yet?" Damon asked.

"Stupid doctors tell us nothing," Andrey said. His accent grew thicker when he was upset.

After Reverend Pat answered her phone and discovered that Spike was in the hospital after a car accident, he and Andrey had brought her here to the hospital while the others stayed behind to tell everyone who arrived what had happened. And to take care of Mr. Fluffy.

Andrey had driven them here, while Reverend Pat had called Damon.

"I'll go find out what is going on," Damon said darkly, setting her down on a chair. "You stay here, sweetheart."

Uh-oh.

When Damon got that look, someone was going to get an earful.

Or worse.

"Do not bother," Andrey told him bitterly. "I threaten them many times. With bodily harm. With cutting of the balls. Choking of the cock. They just stare at me as if I not speak English." He started muttering insults in Russian. "They not know who they deal with. I strangle them until their eyes pop from their sockets."

"Damon," she whispered.

"I'll find out. Don't worry. And I'll keep them from calling the cops on him." He nodded toward Andrey.

"The police do not scare me!" Andrey cried.

Reverend Pat sighed and walked over to talk some sense into Andrey while she sat there anxiously. It seemed to take Damon forever to return. Her phone was buzzing with messages from her friends and their men. But she just couldn't talk to anyone.

When Damon finally came back, she jumped to her feet. The room swayed around her.

Oh God. She was going to be sick. Or faint.

She wasn't sure which.

"Fuck, Millie." She was gathered up against Damon's chest. "It's all right, sweetheart. He's going to be all right. They were doing an MRI on him. I don't know why no one would talk to you, but I think the doctor wanted to check the results before coming to speak to you. The doctor will be here soon."

"He . . . he's alive."

"Of course he is. Do you think a car accident is going to kill him off? He's too stubborn to die. That bastard has nine lives."

She appreciated his attempts to lighten the situation, but the truth was that she felt too upset to smile.

A noise had her turning, tears filling her eyes once more as they all arrived. Sunny and Duke. Jason and Jewel. Betsy and Ink.

They kept coming, filling the room.

Effie and Grady were among the last of them to get there.

Millie was surrounded by friends, all the support she could need, but all she wanted was Spike.

Her best friend. Her Daddy.

The door to the waiting room opened again and a frazzled-looking doctor walked in. He glanced around. "Uh, I'm looking for the family of Quillon Lochlin?"

She jumped up again, breathing through her nausea and dizziness. "Yes? I'm . . . I'm his girlfriend."

"And I'm his brother-in-law," Damon said.

The doctor blinked at them both. His gaze moved over her outfit. Right. She'd forgotten that she had her Easter dress on. Well, screw him if he didn't like it. But he simply turned his gaze to everyone else. "Well, if you could both follow me to my office we can speak alone."

"You can speak here," she said, desperate to hear what he had to say.

"Ahh, the patient's privacy—"

"Just do what she said," Damon demanded, his hand moving to her lower back in support.

"Yes," Andrey yelled. "Do it or I pull your insides out of your ass."

The doctor's eyes widened as he glanced over at Andrey.

"Ignore him," Reverend Pat said, whacking Andrey around the back of his head.

"Right, well, um. As I'm sure you know, Mr. Lochlin was in a car accident. He was rendered unconscious. He's had an MRI and it showed that there is no bleeding on his brain or swelling. He's bruised and sore, but he's now awake and asking for Millie, which I assume is you?"

"Y-yes, that's me. He's really going to be all right?"

The doctor's face softened. "He is. We'll keep him overnight for observation, but I'm confident he'll be able to go home tomorrow. You'll need to keep him quiet for a few days. He shouldn't be stressed or spend too much time on his phone or other screens. His brain needs rest. But yes, he's fine."

"I can . . . can I see him?"

"Uh, yes. But just two people." He eyed everyone in the room again.

"You and Damon go," Grady said to her. "Effie and I will take Reverend Pat and Andrey home."

"We'll all go too," Duke said. "Give you some time with him. But, Millie, you let us know if you need anything, understand?"

She nodded gratefully, waving goodbye to everyone. Damon said goodbye to Effie and Grady. Then he took her hand as they followed the doctor to a private room.

As soon as she stepped into the room, a sob escaped. She tried to hold it back. She really did. The last thing she wanted was to upset Spike. But she just couldn't help it.

Seeing him lying there on the bed, looking so bruised and in pain . . . it was killing her.

"Millie," he groaned.

The room was dark. There was just a small light on in the bathroom. But she could still see that his face was etched tight with pain.

"Oh, Spike," she said quietly.

"Come here, baby doll." He held out his hand and she rushed to his side, taking hold. "I'm all right, baby."

She nodded, aware that there were tears sliding down her face. She had to get herself under control. Had to be brave and strong for him.

It was so freaking hard, though.

This was Spike. The man she loved more than anything.

"Baby doll, you're killing me here," he grumbled.

"Sorry." She wiped at her cheeks with her free hand. "Sorry. I'm good. I'm fine. I was just worried about you when you didn't come back from the airport. And then Andrey and the others turned up in an Uber. Then I got a call from the hospital to say you'd been in a car accident. But when we got there, they wouldn't tell us what was going on. I was just . . . scared."

"Hey, hey, hush. I'm fine," he said in a raspy voice.

Shoot. She had to stop talking. The last thing he needed was her crying and upsetting him. It was time that Millie took care of him rather than the other way around.

So get it together, girl.

"Come here." He tugged at her hand.

She stared down at him, not quite understanding what he wanted. "I am here."

"No, get up on the bed so I can hold you."

Her eyes widened. "Daddy, I can't get on the bed with you."

He was injured. And the bed was tiny. He took up most of the space on it already. There was definitely no room for her even if she wanted to get up on it.

"Baby doll. Up. With. Me."

"Quillon, she's worried about hurting you," Damon said reasonably. "Let her sit in the chair beside you."

Spike looked like he was going to argue.

"Please, Daddy. You've got a concussion and the doctor said you're bruised. I don't want to hurt you further."

"You won't."

"And I don't want to get kicked out of the hospital when they find me lying in the bed with you."

His face darkened. "I'd like to see them try."

Shoot. She wasn't doing well at keeping his stress levels down. Or her own.

"Easy, man," Damon told Spike as he gently pressed her shoulders to get her to sit in the chair. "She just wants to do what's best for you."

"What's best for me is to hold her," Spike grumbled. "She's upset."

"Because she's worried about your ugly mug," Damon shot back.

Spike turned his head toward her, wincing.

"Careful. Don't hurt yourself," she cautioned.

He squeezed her hand. "Baby, you aren't going to hurt me. You could never."

A sob escaped her despite her best efforts to smother it. "I thought you'd died. I didn't know what had happened. Reverend Pat and the others turned up in an Uber and then we got a call for a hospital. I was so scared."

"Fuck, I forgot I was on my way to pick them up. Are they okay?"

"They're fine. You're the one we're all worried about."

"Then stop," he said firmly. "I'm fine."

"You were in a car accident. You have a concussion and bruises."

Damon put his hands on her shoulders, squeezing lightly. Shit. She shouldn't be upsetting Spike. And if he saw she was upset, then he was going to be too.

Taking a deep breath, she worked on calming herself.

So much for taking care of Spike like he did for her.

"Everything is all right now," she said. "You're safe. And I'm going to take care of you."

"Need to take care of you," he countered stubbornly.

"No, Daddy," she said firmly. "You're the one who needs taking care of now."

His gaze narrowed. "I don't think so."

Yeah. She should have known he wouldn't take that well. He was the protector. The nurturer. The one who took care of things.

But he was just going to have to accept that she wanted to do the same for him.

"Fuck," Spike grunted. "Your party."

"It doesn't matter, Daddy."

"It does matter. You worked so hard."

"So I'll have it another weekend. Everyone will understand. All that matters is you."

"Sorry, baby," he said tiredly. "Ruined it."

"You didn't ruin anything," she muttered as he grimaced and shifted position. "All I care about is that you're okay."

"That's all anyone cares about," Damon said firmly. "That you're going to be all right. But you need to listen to the doctors and rest and don't get stressed."

"Millie. Needs looking after."

"I'll do that," Damon said.

Um, she could do that herself.

Pfft. But she didn't argue as she saw Spike drifting off. He needed to get some sleep. That would help him heal.

Thank God he was all right. Because she didn't want to think about her life without him in it.

9

Spike woke up, wincing as knives stabbed at his head.

Fuck, that hurt.

He breathed through the pain, and tried to raise his hand to rub at his temples. Only his hand was stuck. Glancing down, surprise filled him as he saw Millie sleeping on the chair next to his bed.

He frowned.

Where the fuck was he? What was going on and why was Millie sleeping in a fucking chair and not a bed?

Anger filled him as he glanced around, taking in the room.

Fuck. It suddenly came back to him. He'd been in an accident.

Some asshole had run a red light and smashed into his truck.

It could have been worse. So much worse.

And now he was in a hospital bed with his girl sleeping in a fucking chair.

Nope. Not good enough.

Millie needed her sleep. He'd make sure of that once he got them both back home.

Fuck. He just remembered that they had house guests.

Where was Damon? He'd been here last night. Why hadn't he taken Millie home with him?

Suddenly, his girl sat up with a gasp, terror in her face. She glanced around frantically.

Fuck. He hated seeing her like this. So scared.

"Baby doll, it's all right. You're safe. You're okay."

Her gaze went immediately to him, relief filling her face. "Daddy! You're here. I was having a . . . dream . . ." She glanced around and seemed to realize where they were. "It wasn't a dream, was it?"

"No."

She stood, leaning over him. "How do you feel, Daddy? Do you need anything? Water? Your head—"

"Millie," he interrupted her.

"You must need some painkillers," she muttered, ignoring him. "I'll get the nurse."

"Millie," he said more firmly.

"Where's the buzzer? I can't see it. Never mind. Just wait here and I'll go find someone to help you." She brushed back her hair, looking frazzled and unsure.

His baby doll should never have to worry about anything.

"Millie, eyes on me." This time, he kept his voice low and strong. He wasn't going to let her wander off. Who knew what sort of trouble she'd find? With Millie, anything was possible.

Her gaze hit his and he took her in. She looked so damn tired. She was pale with dark marks under her eyes.

"You didn't have any business sleeping the night in a chair," he grumbled.

Fuck. That wasn't what he'd meant to say.

"I couldn't leave you!"

"You should have. You need more sleep. Damon should have made you leave."

She sniffled. "I can't believe you'd be so mean."

What? Why was she so upset? He wasn't trying to be mean, he was looking after her.

"Baby doll, I'm not being mean. You need some proper rest."

"I slept."

"In a chair," he grumbled.

"I wouldn't have slept at home," she told him in a raw voice. "I would have been too worried about you."

Fuck.

She was right. And he was being a grump.

"Sorry, baby. Come here." He held out his hand to her.

She shook her head. "I can't . . . I have to go get the nurse for you."

"Baby. Please. I need to hold you." And he thought she needed that too.

"I shouldn't." But she moved closer and he grabbed her hand, tugging her up onto the bed with him. He gathered her close, his arm around her while she rested her head on his chest.

She yawned. "Oops. Sorry. Tired."

"Just rest, baby," he murmured.

"But I should get the nurse for you."

"I'm fine." He had a killer headache and every movement hurt. But as long as she was all right, then so was he.

It wasn't long until she was breathing more deeply. He had no idea what time it was, but he figured it was still early. So he closed his eyes. He'd just get a few more minutes of sleep.

Spike woke up as someone slipped into his room. A nurse had been in and out all night. It was nearly impossible to get a decent sleep.

He couldn't wait until he was at home. Then he could take

care of his girl better. Spike knew that she was upset by every-thing that had happened. He couldn't even imagine how he would react if he'd been in her shoes, waiting for her to come home and she didn't return.

Yeah. He'd fucking lose it.

So she was holding herself together remarkably well.

However, this time it wasn't a nurse, it was Damon. And he was holding two takeaway coffee cups.

"Where have you been?" Spike grumbled.

Damon raised his eyebrows. "I stayed here all night, but I needed to go home to check on Effie and Grady and shower. Then I figured I'd get some coffee. I didn't really sleep so I need the boost."

Okay, so he hadn't left.

And you're being a grumpy fuck.

Spike grunted. "Sorry. I just don't like that she slept in a chair all night."

"I get it. I got them to bring in a bed." Damon nodded over to a cot that Spike hadn't noticed. "But she kept getting out and sitting next to you. I think she wanted to touch you."

Spike sighed. "Yeah, she can be stubborn."

"Really?" Damon drawled. "Pot, meet kettle."

Spike glowered at him. Asshole. "Give me the coffee."

"These aren't for you. Caffeine isn't good when you have a concussion."

"Who the fuck says?" he demanded, then regretted it when Millie stirred and sat up.

Fuck.

"Baby doll, go back to sleep," he told her in a gentler voice

"I . . . what? I fell asleep? Drat." Her head moved around as she climbed off the bed. "Damon?"

"Hey, sweetheart," Damon said, his entire body softening as he moved over to Millie. "I got you coffee."

"You did?" She reached out and took the coffee cup. "That's why you're my favorite."

"I'm your favorite," Spike grumbled, knowing that he was acting like a jealous ass, but unable to stop himself.

She spun toward him, then tripped. On what, Spike had no idea, but pain flooded him when he attempted to catch her.

Thankfully, Damon grabbed her, managing to keep her upright while still holding his coffee.

"Oh drat! Sorry!" she said. "I tripped."

Spike attempted to breathe through the pain. Fucking hell. It felt like he'd been run over by a train. Then a van. Then another train.

"Over what?" he asked through gritted teeth.

"Nothing. My own stupid feet. Oh, Daddy, are you all right?"

Stupid feet?

Nope. Not having that.

"None of you is stupid," he said. Or he attempted to. But he was also trying not to vomit. So maybe it came out garbled.

Then he felt her cool hand on his face, soothing him. It helped break through the pain. He focused on her touch and not the stabbing agony in his brain.

"Just breathe," she said in a quiet voice. "I'm here. I'm sorry I'm such a klutz. I'll try to be better."

Fuck that.

He wanted her just the way she was.

"You're perfect. Never forget that."

She didn't say anything.

"And I'm keeping track of every time you're down on yourself. There's going to be a reckoning if you keep this up."

"You just concentrate on feeling better."

He could do that. And keep an eye on her.

That was his job.

DAMON TOOK the coffee mug from her hand as he led her to a chair out in the waiting room. Probably a smart idea. She wasn't sure how she hadn't spilled that coffee all over herself when she'd tripped over nothing.

Stupid idiot.

The nurse had come in and kicked them out of Spike's room. Millie didn't understand why she couldn't stay.

"I wanted to stay with him," she said with a small pout.

"I know, sweetheart. But I'm guessing they want to get him into the bathroom."

"So? I could have helped." It wasn't as though he hadn't helped her in the bathroom plenty of times.

"I know," he soothed as he led her to a chair and waited until she'd sat to hand her coffee back to her. "But you know how Spike is. Independent and stubborn."

She snorted. He had that right.

"You know he's going to be a terrible patient, right?" Damon asked as he sat next to her.

Millie took a sip of her coffee. Ahh. Nectar of the Gods. She felt yuck. She needed a shower. A change of clothes. No doubt she looked a fright.

But for now, this coffee would have to suffice.

"I know. I'm going to force him to let me take care of him, though."

"Good luck with that, sweetheart. Maybe you should both move in with me. Until he's feeling better."

She frowned. It was a kind offer. But she wanted to be in her own home, surrounded by her own things. And she was certain that Spike would feel the same way.

"Thanks. But I have this. I can take care of him."

"Not doubting that, Millie," he reassured her. "But who is going to take care of you?"

Surprised filled her at his words. "I can take care of myself. I did it before I met Spike."

"Not to insult you, sweetheart, but you constantly found yourself in trouble before you met him."

"I did not!" She thought that over. "Well, okay, I did a bit. But I have got this. And I'd rather be home. Oh shoot!"

"What is it?" he asked.

"I just remembered that my friends are staying the week with us. I hope they're all right. I wasn't there to show them their bedrooms or cook them dinner. And everything is still outside from the Easter egg hunt."

"Everything is being taken care of," he reassured her. "Effie and Grady went back to your place yesterday after they left here. Duke, Sunny, and some of the others did too. They tidied everything up and made sure your friends settled in all right."

Relief filled her. "Thank you. All of you. I'm so grateful."

"That's what family is for, sweetheart."

10

His girl was running herself ragged.

And Spike fucking hated that.

She needed to rest. To relax. He wasn't even sure that she was sleeping. He tried to stay awake each night to ensure that she lay down beside him and slept, but he kept fucking falling asleep before she did.

They'd been home for three nights now and enough was enough. She was taking care of everyone else and wasn't letting anyone look after her.

Sometimes, he'd wake up and find her sitting next to the bed, just staring at him.

Yeah, the doctor had said that he had to take things easy. But that didn't mean he was a fucking invalid. Today, he was getting up, showering and going downstairs to eat.

Climbing from the bed, he headed into the attached bathroom. After using the toilet and brushing his teeth, he felt a lot better. But his energy was fading fast. Fuck.

Turning on the shower, he stripped out of the boxers he was

wearing and got in. As he started to wash himself the bathroom door opened and Millie ran in.

"Spike!" she cried out, rushing to the shower. Pulling open the door, she stared at him.

She still had dark marks under her eyes, marring her too-pale skin.

She was wearing a pair of pants and a long sweatshirt.

Which he also didn't like. His girl wore dresses. Not pants and sweaters.

Her dark hair was pinned up, flyaway strands falling down.

"What are you doing?" she demanded, her hands on her hips.

He frowned. He didn't mind her calling him Spike or Quillon. But he preferred to be called Daddy.

And it might make him a hypocrite, but he also didn't appreciate her scolding tone.

"I'm Daddy."

She bit her lip, giving him a nervous look. As well she should.

"You're injured," she stated. "You should be in bed."

"I needed a shower."

"Why didn't you call for me?" she fretted, rubbing her hands together. "I could have given you another sponge bath."

That sponge bath would have been enjoyable had she taken care of his hard dick. But she'd refused to, worried that she'd hurt him.

He didn't know how that would even be possible.

Spike ran his hand over his dick, washing it, squeezing it. Her breath caught as she stared down at him.

"Why don't you come in here and bathe me?" he murmured.

"I . . . I really think you should get out," she said, her gaze still on his hand as he stroked himself. "You could get dizzy and fall."

"I'm not dizzy." Well, maybe a little light-headed. But he wasn't telling her that. "Get in here."

She shook her head, stepping back and grabbing a towel. "You come out and I'll dry you off. I made scrambled eggs and toast for breakfast."

Yeah. He didn't like that either. His girl wasn't supposed to touch the stove.

All right, so he knew she wasn't Little all the time. But *he* cooked her meals. That was just the way their dynamic worked.

"Don't worry, I didn't burn anything this time. Reverend Pat helped. He kept an eye on the eggs."

"I'm cooking from now on."

"You have to rest, Spike."

He shot her a look as he finished rinsing off and stepped out. "What do you call me?"

"Daddy." She gulped heavily. "Sorry."

He grunted as she started to dry him. Fuck. What was wrong with him that he hated accepting help? Even from his girl.

"I know that it's hard, but there's nothing wrong with letting me do things for you," she told him as she crouched down to dry his feet and lower legs.

Fuck, she looked good on her knees in front of him. He ran his fingers through her hair, loosening the messy bun. Her hair tumbled around her.

"Beautiful girl," he murmured.

"I love you, Daddy." Her eyes grew wet with tears and he thought she might cry. But closing her eyes, she took in a deep breath and let it out slowly. Opening them, she stared up at him again. "I don't ever want to lose you."

"You won't. I'll always come home to you."

Her lips trembled. "Damon said you're too stubborn to die. And that you have nine lives."

"More," he told her. He owed Damon a lot. The other man had been here every day, trying to help Millie. Effie and Grady had been here a lot too. He knew they'd taken Reverend Pat and the others out several times so that Millie could have a break.

And all of his friends and their girls were checking in on them regularly. Although Duke had told him they were trying not to overwhelm him or Millie, knowing he needed quiet and rest.

They were all good people, and he didn't know what he'd done to deserve them, but he was so thankful that they were in his and Millie's life. That they were taking care of his girl when he couldn't.

She hugged his thighs, her face so close to his dick that he could feel her breath against his cock.

Fuck.

What he wouldn't give to be able to pick her up and carry her to bed. To make love to her like she deserved. Then he'd order her to nap while he took care of everything.

But he couldn't do that.

Millie stood and reaching up, kissed him lightly. "Come to bed. I want to take care of you."

"That's all you've been doing lately. I need to take care of you."

"You always do, Daddy. It's my turn."

He didn't say anything as she took his hand and led him to the bed.

"I'm not going back to bed," he told her firmly. "I'm getting dressed and going downstairs."

"If you get into bed and eat some breakfast, I'll lie with you."

Hmm. She did look like she needed a nap. She helped him into a pair of boxers, then drew back the covers. With sigh, he climbed into bed and patted it. "In you come."

She hesitated, and he gave her a firm look. "In, Millie. Or I'm getting up."

She climbed in, then grabbed the tray, putting it on his lap. "Oh, shoot. It's probably cold."

It had foil over it. He was certain it would be fine. And he didn't want her going anywhere.

"It's fine," he said gruffly, lifting the foil.

Huh, the eggs really did look like they hadn't been burned. Millie reached for the fork.

Good.

She was going to eat. He had yet to see her eat these last few days. But instead of feeding herself, she offered the food to him.

Oh, hell no.

No way was she feeding him. He took the fork from her, ignoring her look of surprise, and held the eggs to her lips. "Eat."

"I'm not hungry."

He pressed the food into her mouth, not buying that for a second. Or she might think she wasn't hungry, however she still needed to eat.

Her stomach gurgled, and he raised an eyebrow at her. "You're not looking after yourself properly, Millie."

"I'm meant to be looking after you."

He fed her another bite of food. "Not at the expense of your health."

"I'm fine, Spike. You're the one who was injured and in the hospital. You need more rest and care."

What he needed was his girl in his arms each night. He needed to look after her.

"Please eat something," she begged.

"I'll eat and I'll even stay in bed a few more hours if you do something for me."

She eyed him suspiciously. "What?"

"Stay in bed with me and have a nap."

"I said I'd lie with you. But I can't stay in bed for long. I have to go clean up the breakfast mess. Sunny and Betsy are taking Mrs. Larsen and Mrs. Spain shopping and I have to make sure they're ready. And Andrey, Mr. Spain, and Reverend Pat are going out with Damon to do something. Hopefully, he's not taking them to Pinkies, I don't think Reverend Pat would understand."

"He'd be fine with it. You think he doesn't know about who Damon is and what he does?"

"Oh. He does?"

"Yeah. But Damon won't be going there at this time of the morning. And they can all get themselves ready. Now, do we have a deal?"

She gave him a pouting look, then she sighed. "Fine."

"Fine, what?"

"Fine, Daddy," she said in a softer voice.

"That's better." He fed her and himself until he felt a wave of fatigue wash over him. After putting the tray on the bedside table, he lay down and drew her in against his chest.

"Fuck, you feel good in my arms," he told her.

"You feel good too, Daddy." Her hand reached down and brushed his half-hard cock. "Do you want me to . . ."

"Only if you want to, baby doll," he told her, needing the taste of his girl on his lips. "But first you're going to ride my face."

"I can't do that."

"Sure you can." He pushed himself further down the bed so his head was off his pillow. "Get those clothes off, then straddle my face and feed me that delicious pussy."

"Spike, I can't!"

"Why not?"

"Because you're injured."

"My mouth isn't injured. Besides, I feel a lot better." Okay, sometimes his head still felt like he was being stabbed by a knife and his body was bruised and battered. But he'd been in worse states.

It wasn't going to stop him from eating his girl's pussy until she screamed.

"But your head is."

"I won't move it."

"I'm too . . . I can't get over you like that . . . what if I slip? Fall? What if I suffocate you?"

"Millie," he growled. "That just earned you a spanking."

"What? Why?"

He couldn't believe that she was giving him an incredulous look. She knew why she'd just earned a spanking.

"As soon as I'm feeling completely better, you're going over my lap for a spanking."

"Nooo! Daddy, that's not fair."

"Did I not warn you what would happen if you kept speaking badly about yourself?"

"Yes . . . but . . . I wasn't really talking badly about myself."

"You were worried about suffocating me," he grumbled at her. "Why'd you say that? What were you thinking about yourself?"

"That . . . well . . . I . . ." Her shoulders slumped. "Daddy, I don't want to hurt you."

"No way that's happening." But fuck, he felt awful because now she looked so sad and upset. And not like she would enjoy herself.

So he carefully sat up and patted his lap. "Come here. Straddle my legs."

He held out his hand and helped her climb back onto the bed. Then he cupped her face with his large hands.

"I love you, my precious girl. I don't want you thinking or saying bad things about yourself."

"I know."

He ran his thumb over her lips. "Fuck, I want to taste you."

"You do?"

"Yeah, nothing more delicious than my girl's pussy."

"Daddy!" she cried, blushing. "I would like that, but I'm scared about you getting hurt."

"I know you are. But maybe I could have a small taste." He leaned in and kissed her. He kept it slow and gentle.

For both of their sakes.

When he drew back, they were both breathing heavily and he was as hard as a rock.

"Let me take care of you?" she whispered. "Please?"

"Fuck, baby. Can't say no to that. But I need you to get naked. I want to see your breasts. To touch your pussy."

She carefully climbed off him and started to strip. He watched her carefully, hungrily.

Then he laid down again once she was fully naked. "Come here, baby. Climb on top of me."

She moved hesitantly, but slid her leg over his waist.

"That's my good girl. Now feed me your breast."

Her entire face was red, but she leaned down with her breast cupped, holding it to his mouth. He sucked on her nipple, tonguing it, biting down gently until she was crying out, her need clear on her face.

He tapped her thigh, and she moved her other breast over so it could get the same treatment. As he teased her nipple, he ran his fingers up her thigh, then pressed them between his stomach and her pussy. She rose up on her knees, giving him access to play with her clit, to thrust his fingers deep into her pussy.

Finally, he pushed her carefully back.

"Turn around, baby doll. Take my dick into your mouth."

"You won't overdo anything," she said sternly.

"I won't. I promise."

She moved so carefully it made his teeth ache. He wanted to

spin her around, to bring her hips back so he could devour her. But he knew that she'd stop everything and he really needed to come.

When she was in position and her pussy was exposed to his gaze and his fingers, she tugged down his boxers and took him into her mouth.

Fuck. Him.

He wasn't going to last long. He sucked in a breath, trying to control himself.

Parting her pussy lips, he pressed two fingers into her as he finger-fucked her.

"So wet for me, aren't you, baby doll?" he murmured. "Do you like my cock in your mouth?"

She hummed around his dick and it was nearly his undoing. A shaft of pain hit him as he moved his head and he had to breathe through it.

He was fine.

This was what he wanted.

She sucked on him harder as he drew his fingers to his mouth and licked them clean.

"God, you taste so damn good, baby doll. Fuck. Me." He groaned as he played with her clit. "Come for me. That's a good girl. Let me hear you come."

Spike hoped that none of their house guests were walking past their door as she let out a scream of pleasure as she found her release. He drove his fingers into her pussy, feeling her tighten around him.

Fuck. Yes.

He removed his fingers, thrusting them into his mouth.

God. So good.

She took him deep into her throat and then swallowed.

Hell.

It was too much.

"I'm gonna come. Drink all of me down. Don't miss a drop. Be a good girl for me."

He came with a moan, ignoring the ache in his body and head. Fuck, it felt like he wasn't going to stop. Finally, he relaxed back, letting out a deep breath.

That felt so fucking good.

"Such a good girl . . . my good, good girl," he mumbled as he drifted off to sleep.

MILLIE slowly and carefully climbed off Spike, standing next to the bed. She watched him for a long moment. Should she pull up his boxers? Seemed uncomfortable to sleep like that, but she didn't want to wake him.

Instead, she drew the blankets up over him before she headed into the bathroom to get cleaned up.

Once she was clean and dressed, she grabbed the tray of food and tiptoed out of the room. A wave of dizziness hit her at the top of the stairs. And she had to sit abruptly before she passed out.

Traversing stairs wasn't her talent on the best of days, let alone when she was operating on limited sleep, food, and a bucket load of stress.

Unfortunately, that was when Damon found her.

Crap.

"Oh, hi!" She waved down at him as he stood at the base of the stairs, staring up at her sternly.

"Good morning."

"I didn't realize you were here yet."

"Sunny and Betsy just left with Mrs. Spain and Mrs. Larsen," he told her. "I'm here for the men. They're getting ready."

"Oh good. I appreciate you taking them, Damon."

"You know what you can do to thank me?"

She frowned. "What?" Did he need something from her? Because she wasn't sure that she had anything else in her tank left to give.

"You can take a nap. Eat something. Rest."

"Damon—"

"I mean it, Millie," he said in a firm voice. "If you don't start taking care of yourself the way I know Quillon would want, then I'm taking over."

"What does that mean?" she asked.

"It means that all of you will be coming to stay with me and I will make sure that you rest and eat and don't run yourself into the ground."

"You're not my Daddy," she muttered.

"Just think of me as Uncle Damon," he countered.

"Kind of disturbing."

"I know why you're sitting there, Millie," he said.

He did not.

Did he?

"And I'm putting my foot down. No more. Understand? You have to take care of yourself. You can't pour from an empty cup."

"Hear, hear!"

She turned to find Reverend Pat behind her.

"You tell her, young man."

Okay. Reverend Pat calling Damon Steele a young man was pretty hilarious. Or it would have been if she wasn't upset with Damon right now.

Reverend Pat took the tray from her.

"Reverend Pat," she protested. "I can do that."

"No, you can go get into bed and have a nap," he replied. "We'll be out of the house most of the day and when we get back, Andrey is cooking."

"That's right, I am," Andrey boomed from behind Reverend

Pat. He took the tray off the older man before heading downstairs.

"Does he know how to cook?" she whispered.

"No idea," Reverend Pat replied. "But we're going to find out. Now, off you go and rest."

She heaved herself onto her feet. Maybe she'd just nap. For a few minutes.

11

F uck. He'd fallen asleep again.

Spike let out a deep sigh as he stared up at the ceiling. Where was his girl? Had she fallen asleep? He glanced around, scowling as he found her asleep in the fucking armchair in the corner. Mr. Fluffy was sleeping on the floor in front of her.

What the hell?

Why wasn't she sleeping with him?

Getting up, he used the bathroom quickly and got dressed before standing in front of her. Could he lift her up? Would he wake her?

Damn it. She wasn't sleeping there.

He'd wake her up in a minute. First, he searched out his phone. She'd hidden it, but he knew all her hiding places. He found it in her underwear drawer.

There were several messages that he went through, finally reading the latest one from Damon.

. . .

DAMON: *I've taken the men away for the day. I'll keep them out late. Make sure Millie rests. I found her sitting at the top of the stairs, pale and shaking. Didn't like it. Told her that if she doesn't look after herself that I'm bringing you all to stay with me and I'll take care of her.*

LIKE FUCK HE WOULD. Spike appreciated him looking out for his girl.

But that was Spike's job.

SPIKE: *I have her. Appreciate your help. Not needed.*

RIGHT. It was time for things to change.

MILLIE WOKE up as she was jostled.

"Nooo, I don't wants to go to school today."

A chuckle hit her ears. "No school for you, baby doll."

"Oh good. Wants to sleep."

"That's good, since that's all you're doing today."

Wait. Who was that?

As she was placed down on her back, she opened her eyes, staring up into Spike's worried face. She smiled.

"Daddy! I loves you."

"I love you too."

Then she frowned at how pale he looked. Suddenly, she realized that she was in bed. She hadn't gone to sleep in the bed.

With a gasp, she sat up. "You carried me!"

"Yeah. Because you were sleeping in a damn chair. That's not happening, baby doll."

"I didn't want to disturb you," she said worriedly. She knew how he felt about her sleeping in chairs. "And you shouldn't be carrying me."

"I'm fine," he told her.

Sure he was. Only problem was, he was pale and looked like he was in pain.

"Right now, the person I'm worried most about is you," he added.

"Me? But Daddy, I'm good. I wasn't in a car accident. I don't have a concussion."

"But you're running yourself ragged. You're exhausted and you're going to end up with a migraine or passing out if you continue. Then you'll be in the hospital."

"That won't happen."

"Damon texted me."

"Rats. That tattletale. Wait until I see him again." She thumped her fist against her hand. "Snitches get stitches."

"He did the right thing and you know it." He pointed a finger at her. "You're spending the day in bed."

"What? I can't!"

He crossed his arms over his chest and gave her a stubborn look.

Drat.

"I have to get your lunch. Do the dishes. The washing. And we have guests."

"Guests who aren't here and can take care of themselves. And everything else I'm capable of doing."

Mr. Fluffy let out a woof as though in agreement.

"Whose side are you on?"

The dog yawned and rolled onto his back.

"Traitor."

"Mr. Fluffy knows what is good for you. Now, I'm going to get you a onesie and a bottle. You can watch TV, read, or sleep. Those are your choices."

"But you can't go down the stairs on your own," she protested.

What if he got dizzy?

Spike turned to look at her. "No."

No?

What did that mean?

"You are not the boss. Daddy is. No fretting or worrying over me anymore."

"But . . . but . . . I nearly lost you." She didn't mean to say that. It just sort of slipped out. But it was the truth. "And I have to take care of you. Because I don't want anything to happen to you."

His face grew soft and he walked over to her, kneeling on the floor beside her. Then he cupped her face with his hands.

"I know. And if I could erase all your worries, I would. But I'm all right. I'm here. I'm not going anywhere."

"I just . . . I get scared sometimes. When it hits me. Keeping busy helps me to forget."

"Oh, baby doll." He wrapped his arms around her waist and she patted his head before she started massaging his shoulders.

He groaned. "That feels good."

"Yeah? I could give you a massage."

Leaning back, he glared up at her. "Nice try. I'm looking after you."

"But you're always looking after me. I just . . . I want to take care of you too."

"Looking after you makes me happy. I can't relax knowing you're running yourself ragged. So you being happy and healthy is the best medicine for me."

"There's some more Daddy logic," she grumbled.

"But it's working, isn't it?"

"Kind of," she admitted. "Just promise me . . . promise me you'll always be here. That I won't to lose you."

"I promise. I will always be here. Always be yours. Just like you are mine."

FUCK.

This was harder than he'd thought. He'd managed to going up and down the stairs to get Millie a bottle. He'd even put her in a onesie. But when he'd headed back downstairs, he'd had to sit and rest.

And he was still sitting on the sofa, resting.

He heard the front door opened and he glanced over as Damon walked into the living room.

"What are you doing here?" Spike asked.

"Nice to see you too." Damon eyed him before taking a seat in an armchair opposite him. "What're you doing?"

"Just thought I'd go run a marathon."

"Good plan," Damon replied.

Spike closed his eyes, rubbing his forehead. "I feel like shit."

"Not surprising. You were in a fucking car accident."

There was something in the other man's voice. Concern? Anger?

Spike stared over at him as Damon glowered at him. "I know."

"Yeah, you know. Do you have any idea, though, what it would do to the rest of us if something happened to you?"

Fuck. He hadn't even thought about how Damon would feel about all this. How it might be affecting him.

"I didn't do it on purpose," he pointed out.

"Well, don't do it again."

"I'll try not to." Spike's lips twitched. "Especially if you're gonna go all mother hen on me all the time."

"Mother hen?" Damon asked. "You won't let me help with anything, asshole."

"We're fine."

"You're not fine. You're injured and you need time and rest to recover. And Millie is running herself ragged trying to give you that."

"I'm taking care of Millie," he told him.

"Good. Then let the rest of us take care of everything else. Let me help you, Quillon. You can't look after her if you're dead on your feet. You're not a fucking superhero. You need help. I'm here offering help."

Fuck it.

"Family helps each other. And we're family, right?"

Spike sighed. Bastard had him over a barrel and he knew it. Spike needed help, he just really didn't want to admit it.

"All right. You can help but only because Millie needs me."

"Of course. Because of Millie. So, tell me what needs doing." Damon stood.

"Yeah, all right." He sighed. "Damon?"

"Yep?"

"Thanks, man. I appreciate the help."

"You'd do the same for me," Damon replied.

Yeah, he would. Because that's what you did for family.

12

"Okay, Daddy, I think everything is sorted for tomorrow. Everyone is coming. The weather looks good. You'll set up the tables and I'll decorate. And all the outfits are ready."

Mr. Fluffy looked up at her from where he lay in his dog bed.

"Yes, your outfit has been cleaned, Mr. Fluffy. I can't believe how dirty you got it last time. You barely move, how did it end up so filthy?"

Spike snorted out a laugh. "I have some idea."

"I can't understand why he doesn't like being dressed up like a rabbit."

Three weeks had passed since the car accident and Spike was feeling nearly as good as new. Sometimes, he got tired and had to rest. But his bruises had healed and he was doing so much better.

Millie was so relieved. She was still finding it hard to let him out of her sight still, but he'd been out a few times without her and she'd managed.

Sort of.

She'd gotten sick from running herself into the ground, ending up with a bad cold. Spike had taken care of her, of course. And thankfully, she hadn't passed it on to anyone else.

"And Duke and Razor are going to pick everyone up?"

"Yes," he said. "They'll go to the airport and collect them on the way."

Thank God. She really hadn't wanted Spike to go to the airport to get her friends again.

"That's it then. Nothing else left to do until tomorrow."

"There's one more thing to do," he said, looking across the room at her.

He got up off his chair and walked over to where she sat on the sofa.

"What is it?" she asked.

"We have to take care of the punishment you earned, baby doll."

"Daddy! I never earned a punishment. Millie is a good girl."

"Of course she is. But she also earned a spanking."

"Woof," Mr. Fluffy said.

She glared down at the dog. "Whose side are you on?"

"Mine," Spike said. "Because he wants to take care of you like I do. Now, stand up."

She stood and he sat in her place before pulling her over his lap.

Well, shoot.

She was already in her dinosaur pajamas. They were white with little dancing dinosaurs all over them. He grabbed them, lowering them, then her panties.

Until her poor bottom was exposed and defenseless.

"Remember, Daddy, I've gots to go on a hunt tomorrow. You can'ts spank me too much or too hard."

"I'll always spank you just the right amount, baby doll."

Yeah. She wasn't sure that made her feel better.

His hand landed on her ass and she let out a cry.

Ouchie!

"I know you can handle a lot more than that."

Drat. She'd thought if she'd started yelling straight away then perhaps he'd go easy on her.

No such luck.

His hand landed over and over again, not stilling until she was a snotty, sobbing mess on his lap. Then he rubbed her lower back soothingly until she'd stopped crying.

After pulling up her panties and pajama pants, he settled her on his lap, facing him. Reaching over, he grabbed a tissue and wiped her face. She blew into it, clearing her nose.

Gross.

"Baby doll, you mean every-fucking-thing to me. Never want to hear you speak badly about yourself, understand?" he asked gruffly as he ran his hand up and down her back.

"I understand, Daddy."

He drew her against his chest, hugging her tight. "Good girl. I have something for you. Although this might not be the best time to give it to you."

She leaned back to give him a suspicious look. "Is it another spanking, Daddy?"

"Have you done something to deserve another spanking?" He raised his eyebrows.

"Nope. Nuh-uh. No freaking way."

"Then you don't have to worry about another spanking, do you?"

She sighed. "Sadly, I've always got to be on the watch for the next spanking. They're sneaky things."

"If you did as Daddy said and followed all the rules, then you wouldn't have to worry about spankings."

"Pfft. Sounds boring."

He shook his head at her. Then he set her on her feet and stood, holding out his hand. Millie followed him into his office.

Letting go of her hand, he pointed at the floor. "Stay here."

Sheesh. So bossy.

He moved around his desk and unlocked one of the drawers. She couldn't see what he was doing over the wide desk, but when he returned he held a small black box in his hand.

Her heart skipped a beat, her stomach going all funny as he dropped down onto one knee.

"Spike," she whispered.

"Millie, you're the best part of me. The light in my life. I wasn't really living until you came along, I was simply existing. Getting through the days. But you taught me that life is worth living. Every day, you make me smile with your enthusiasm, your humor, the way you enjoy every minute of every day. I love you. I want to be your man, your Daddy, and your husband for the rest of our lives. Will you have me?"

She dropped to her knees in front of him, tears dripping down her face, nodding.

"Baby?"

"I . . . I . . . y-yes!"

He opened the ring box, revealing the most gorgeous ring. It had a square pale green stone in the center surrounded by small diamonds.

Spike slid it onto her finger, before she threw herself at him, hugging him.

"Shh, baby. It's all right."

"I'm j-just so happy! I'm going to be y-yours."

"You always have been. You've always been my girl. My very best girl."

13

Spike smiled as he watched Millie bustling around. She'd worked so hard to make today happen. She'd worried about whether it was silly to do it four weeks after Easter and he'd told her that it didn't matter when it happened. As long as it was something she wanted.

She looked so happy. So excited.

Fuck. She was his everything.

He'd do anything to keep that smile on her face.

Although he was putting his foot down when it came to wearing the damn bunny suit.

Not happening. No way.

"She looks so happy."

He glanced down as Reverent Pat joined him. The older man was still fit and active, but Spike was worried about when the day came that Millie would have to say goodbye to her friends.

However, today wasn't that day.

Spike grunted. A couple of dogs raced past, tugging at a rope toy. Hatter and Bandit. Luna followed them, barking.

Spike looked around for Mr. Fluffy only to find him sitting in the shade of one of the tables.

A sigh escaped him. Mr. Fluffy was the problem child of the group. Anti-social, he never joined in with any of the other dogs and Spike had given up trying to make him.

"I hope she is," he finally replied, realizing that Reverent Pat was waiting for a reply.

"Well, if she wasn't, boy, you'd have to answer to me."

Spike bit back a smile at the older man's threat. It was ridiculous, but he respected him more for it.

"How does this hunting the eggs work?" Andrey asked in his loud voice as he came up beside him. "Do we shoot them? Where are the guns?"

Reverend Pat gave the other man a look of disgust. "Don't pretend that you don't know how an Easter egg hunt works."

"Me? How would I know?"

"Because you're not an idiot," Mrs. Larsen said as she wandered up, using her walking stick. Andrey immediately held out his hand for her to take to help keep her steady.

Spike needed to get some more chairs down here for them all. He glanced over as Millie burst into laughter. She was standing with Sunny, Betsy, and Jewel. By the table that held the baskets stood Emme, Dahlia, and Tabby. They were trying on the headbands that Millie had made them.

Mr. and Mrs. Spain were in a conversation with Livvy, Sav, Greer, and Livvy's nephews who were also doing the Easter egg hunt. Thankfully, Buster had left his rabbit, Cinnabun, at home.

Baron and Royal came up to the boys. Baron put Buster up on his shoulders, while Royal took hold of Wyatt. Ethan followed along behind them.

Most of the men were standing on the edges, watching over their families. He knew that Millie had invited Brody, Autumn, and the Fox. Well, she'd sent an invitation to Brody through Ink.

However, he didn't expect them to turn up. The only people they were waiting for were Effie, Damon, and Grady. Plus Brooks, Effie's nephew, who had become good friends with Royal and Baron.

"And how do you know I'm not?" Andrey asked. "Wait. Are you saying I am an idiot or am not an idiot? I'm confused."

Mrs. Larsen snorted. "I think that answers your question. Spike, dear, could you get an old lady a glass of that fairy juice?"

"Of course." He walked away to grab a glass as his phone pinged, letting him know someone was waiting at the gate. Odd. Damon had the code. All of his friends did. Surprise filled him as he spotted the driver of the vehicle.

Brody.

Fuck. Was the Fox coming? Autumn was sitting in the passenger seat and he couldn't see anyone else. He doubted the Fox would let Brody drive if he was with him. But who knew how that man's brain worked?

Spike let them in, watching as Steele's car pulled in behind them.

Well, this was going to be interesting.

Grabbing a glass of pink fairy juice, he took it back to Mrs. Larsen. "Here. I'll get you a seat."

"Yes, I might need a seat after I add a bit of my own special juice to this." She drew a flask out of her one-of-a-kind Spain bag. Spike thought the bags that Mrs. Spain created were kind of . . . interesting.

But what did he know about fashion?

"Mrs. Larsen!" Reverend Pat said in a shocked voice. "What do you think you are doing?"

"What?" Mrs. Larsen said. "It's for medicinal purposes."

"What is?" Mr. Spain asked loudly as he and Mrs. Spain joined them. "Oh, is that your special flask? Can I have some?"

"No, you can't have any," Mrs. Spain replied.

"Why not?"

"Because last time you had some of that special juice, you ended up line-dancing!"

And that was bad?

Spike gave Mrs. Spain a confused look.

"Naked!" she added.

Spike grimaced. Hmm. Yeah. That wouldn't be good. For anyone.

"Excuse me, I have to go greet some guests. I'll get some chairs for you all." He stopped to speak to Razor and Ink, asking them to bring some more seats down.

Then he grabbed Millie. "Baby, more guests have arrived."

"Effie?" Millie asked.

Effie and Millie had become good friends. But then, everyone who met Millie fell in love with her.

"Yeah. But also Brody and Autumn."

Millie's eyes widened before a large smile came over her face. "They came? That's awesome!"

Spike grunted.

"Daddy, don't be rude to them."

"Not going to be rude to them."

"It's good that they came," she said. "It can't be easy for them, being attached to our furry friend."

"Furry friend?" he asked.

"Yes, well, I don't like to say his name out loud."

"Wise," he grunted. "Pretty sure he's like Rumpelstiltskin."

"Exactly what I thought, Daddy!" she cried, clapping her hands. "Great minds think alike."

SPIKE SENT HER A LOOK. Millie knew he was just worried, and he didn't mean to look as though he'd been sucking on a lemon. She didn't know Brody and Autumn well, but Brody was good friends with a lot of them. And Autumn was fast becoming one of Sunny's closest friends.

Leaving them out just because they were with the Fox wasn't nice.

And frankly, she thought leaving the Fox out was mean too. After everything he'd done for all of them . . . well, he deserved an Easter egg hunt, too.

Spike was just being a worrywart. He did that sometimes.

But nothing bad was going to happen. It was Easter! Well, a month after Easter but in her mind it was Easter. It was impossible for bad things to happen at this time of year.

Millie followed Spike through the house to the front door. Brody and Autumn were already out of the car, looking around. Brody saw them and waved.

Steele, Grady, Effie, and Brooks pulled up behind them. She waved at them before she headed down to Brody and Autumn, who looked like they were contemplating climbing back into their car.

"Hi, guys! I'm so glad you made it!" She wrapped her arms around Brody first, since she knew him better. Then Autumn. Millie wanted them to feel welcomed here.

Spike was so close behind her that she could feel the heat of him. Protective, as always.

"Sorry we're late," Autumn said with a shy smile.

"My fault," Brody added. "Apparently, I drive like a myopic grandpa."

"I didn't say that!" Autumn protested.

He just grinned at her.

"Well, I'm so glad you're here for Millie's Super-Duper Easter Egg hunt!"

Brody blushed. "Um, us too."

"Did you, um, come alone?" Millie asked.

"Millie," Spike warned.

"What?" She glanced over her shoulder, giving him an innocent look.

He gave her a knowing look back. Drat.

"It's okay," Autumn said quickly. "It's just the two of us. Is that okay?"

"Of course it is!" Millie said, clapping her hands. "Just like it's okay if all of you had wanted to come. Everyone is welcome. My house is your house. Go out back. Everyone is here. There are baskets and headbands and yummy snacks. Try the cupcakes! I ate two." She patted her tummy.

"Two?" Spike asked. "I thought I told you one."

"Maybe that's what you thought you told me, Daddy. But that's not what I heard."

He leaned into her to whisper. "Baby doll, you're close to having your bottom warmed. No more cupcakes."

"Yes, Daddy."

Yikes.

Autumn and Brody quickly headed off.

"I hope you didn't scare them, Daddy," she said worriedly, turning to look at him.

"Baby doll, they're in love with the Fox. I doubt anything I could do could scare them."

Well, she guessed that was true.

"Was that who I think it was?" Steele demanded as he walked up to them.

"Damon!" Millie cried, throwing her arms around Spike's brother-in-law.

"Hey, Millie," Damon said in a softer voice as he wrapped his arms around her. "Thanks for inviting us."

"Of course! You're family." She drew back to smile up at him.

Then Spike cleared his throat and tugged at her. "Want to let my girl go?"

"Not really." Damon grinned at Spike.

She sighed. Silly men.

"Well, you have to, because I want a cuddle," Grady said, stealing her from Damon to wrap her in a tight hug.

She was so glad they'd both found Effie. They seemed so much lighter. They smiled. And even though there was still darkness in their eyes, it seemed to lighten around the blonde bombshell.

Millie turned to give Effie, then Brooks, a hug.

"Come on! It's time for the hunt to begin. Oh, first we need the Easter Bunny to hide the eggs." She gave Spike a look.

He just shook his head at her. "No way."

"Please, Daddy," she pleaded. "Someone has to do it."

"Yeah, well, it's not going to be me. Not. Happening."

14

"Okay, everyone listen to the rules. The Easter Bunny is currently hiding all of the Easter eggs for us to hunt. You all get a basket and you can go by yourself or with friends to find the eggs. But no Daddies are allowed to help."

She gave the Daddies a stern look while her friends all giggled.

Silly Spike had pretended that he didn't want to get dressed in the giant bunny suit that she'd made for him. But he secretly loved it.

"All of the dogs are inside," Razor called out as he joined them.

"Thank you," she replied. "We don't want any dogs eating chocolate. Now, when you're finished you can come back here and eat as many Easter eggs as you want. No one is allowed to stop you."

Damon grinned. "I don't think that's an official rule."

"Is too! I wrote it in my official Super-Duper Easter Egg hunt notebook."

"Well, I'll have to ask Spike about that," Damon said.

"No need to do that. You know what snitches get." She pointed at Damon menacingly.

Yeah, he looked suitably impressed.

As he should be.

"Right! The Easter Bunny should be about finished. Let's go find some eggs!" she cried.

Whoops and hollers as well as laughter followed her as she led the way through the trees.

Huh. That was weird. Millie looked around. Where were the eggs? Where was Daddy hiding them?

"Um, Millie?"

She glanced over at Betsy, who held up a carrot. Then to Tabby, who was holding a potato. And Autumn, who had a parsnip?

What the heck?

"Easter Bunny! Easter Bunny!" she yelled.

She stormed off, ignoring her friends calling out to her to stop and wait for them. She caught sight of someone in the distance. A fluffy tail.

It didn't quite look like a bunny tail. But it had to be Spike.

"Easter Bunny! Come back here! Where are our eggs and why are you leaving veggies!"

She ran off, aware that her friends were catching up.

"There he is!" He was crouched down, picking up their yummy eggs. "Get him, Littles!"

"Wait!" Brody called out. "That's no bunny."

Millie's eyes widened as she took in the image. "It's . . . it's a fox!"

They all took a collective breath in and she turned to look at Autumn and Brody as they stared at each other.

"Daddy!" Autumn said.

Brody nodded. "Papa."

The person in the fox costume . . . was actually the Fox?

Ooh, that trickster.

"I don't care who he is, he's stealing our chocolate!" Millie cried. "Let's get him!"

Sunny and Betsy held her back.

"Let me at him!"

"What's all this yelling?" Spike rushed up to them, the other Daddies with him. He had changed out of his costume.

"There's a fox in these woods," she told him. "And he's a chocolate egg stealer."

Spike's eyes widened. "What? A fox?"

"The Fox," Emme said with a frown. "But why is he stealing our eggs? Fox! Bring them back or I'm not going to be happy."

"Same!" Sunny said with a frown.

"What the hell is going on?" Spike asked.

"Daddy!" Autumn called out. "Can you hear us? We want our eggs. Not veggies!"

"He left veggies?" Reyes asked. "That's not weird at all."

"All Little girls and boys need more veggies," a voice said as a man in a fox costume stepped out of the woods, holding a basket filled with chocolate eggs.

Their chocolate eggs!

"Get him!" she cried, pointing at him.

Spike wrapped an arm around her waist, pulling her up against him. Her feet were off the ground as she kicked her legs out as though she was running.

"Daddy! Let me go!"

"Nope. Not happening."

"Fox, what are you doing?" Duke asked.

"Just trying to save their teeth and the sugar high," the Fox replied. "I thought you'd all be happy with me? No?"

"Daddy, no!" Autumn stomped her foot.

"Hmm. Strange. You don't want veggies instead of chocolate?" the Fox asked.

"We don't." There was a small smile on Brody's face.

"Then I guess you'll just have to follow me!" The Fox took off, chocolate eggs falling from the basket as he ran.

Everyone stood there for a moment, then Autumn ran after him with a cry. "Chocolate!"

"Sorry, Millie." Brody turned to her with a wince. "He didn't mean to ruin anything. Autumn was . . . well, she was sad he wasn't coming. And I think this is his weird way of joining in. I hope he didn't mess it all up?"

Millie grinned. "Actually, no. I think this actually made it better."

"It did?" Brody shoved his glasses up his nose. "Really?"

"Uh-huh. Rescuing our eggs from a fox? Now, that's an Easter egg hunt! Let's go, Littles!" She raised her fist in the air and she would have taken off after the Fox if Spike wasn't holding her.

"You really think this is safe?" he asked.

She glanced up at him to see him staring at Duke, then Brody, and Markovich.

"I think it's more than safe," Markovich replied. "He would do anything to keep these two safe. And Sunny and Emme. This is him . . . having fun, I believe."

"All right," Spike said, loosening his hold on her. "Then go get your eggs!"

Millie whooped and raced off. This was so much fun!

"Daddy, can you believe how many eggs I got?" Millie stared at them all laid out on the coffee table.

"I'm sure there are more there than I put out in the first

place," Spike grumbled from where he sat on the sofa behind her.

Yeah, Millie thought so too. Which meant the Fox had brought some with him.

So he hadn't really thought they wanted veggies instead of eggs.

Yuck!

She put all the eggs back into the basket and got to her feet. Reverend Pat and the others had all gone to bed. So it was just her, Spike, and Mr. Fluffy up. Well, Mr. Fluffy was asleep.

She curled up into Spike's lap, and he tightened his arms around her. "Good day, baby doll?"

"The best, Daddy."

"Good, I'm glad." He kissed the top of her head.

"I can't wait to do it again next year."

If she heard him groan, she was going to ignore it. Daddy would do it all over again if it made her happy.

Because he was the best Daddy ever.

Made in the USA
Las Vegas, NV
09 May 2024